MOMMY'S GIRL

THE HARRIET HIGH SERIES

Printed in the United States of America

Cover Design: Independent Designer

Formatting & Consulting:
LPW Editing & Consulting Services, LLC
The Editorial Midwife Publishing
www.litapward.com

First Printing, 2020

ISBN – 13: 978-1-7343853-3-5

Books by Yolanda

For Teens:

Harriet High Series

❖ *Mysteries of Harriet High:*
The Secret of Twila Anderson

❖ *Twila's Dilemma:*
Field of Lies, Touchdown in Truth

❖ *Summer Rain*

For ADULTS:

Wolf in Sheep's Clothing

Eyes of the Enemy

MOMMY'S GIRL

YOLANDA RANDOLPH

THE HARRIET HIGH SERIES

PROLOGUE

T he time is here," Raven Mayz thought quietly to herself while glancing around at the machinery that surrounded her. Tubes and wires of all different shapes and sizes hung loosely on the wall behind her. A big monitor hung on the wall directly beside her; it beeped every few minutes. Paying the most attention to the electronic fetal monitoring that was attached to her belly, she smiled. Looking over at her sleeping boyfriend, well, a boy who she wanted to be her boyfriend, Shannon, she gave him a quick smile and then turned towards one of the floor's nurse assistants, Leandra, who had walked in a few minutes before.

"These are for you!" she squealed while placing a small bouquet of yellow and white flowers on the counter.

"Thanks," Raven said and sat up a little further in bed. "Who are they from?"

"Uh, looks like they are from the staff at Harriet High."

"Oh, okay." Disappointed, Raven had hoped that the gift was from her mother or any member of her family for that matter.

"They don't care at all," she quipped and rubbed her stomach.

"Nice flowers and it was nice of your school to send them to you."

"Yeah."

"Well, you know to call me if you need anything. Do you have your call bell?"

Raven uncomfortably looked around for the device that had become one of her best friends, the good ole call bell. All she had to do was push the button and she got whatever she needed or wanted. Not only her, but Shannon too. So much better that what I get at home, she said when she was first introduced to it. Finally, some attention, she thought quietly to herself as the nurses were checking her in and hooking her up to all the machines. "Yep, right here."

"Okay, cool. Push it if you need anything. Do you want some ice chips? Is your mouth dry?"

"Nah," Raven replied but stopped as a small contraction was building up within her wound. "I'm good," she managed to get out before the contraction moved to its worse stage.

"Okay, what about your boyfriend? Should I get him a blanket?"

Raven looked over at Shannon and shook her head. "No, I think he's good."

"Okay," Leandra smiled and walked out of the room, gently closing the door behind her.

Raven looked around and sighed. "Almost here baby girl," she whispered soothingly and looked down at her belly. "Ow," she winced out in pain as another harsh contraction took over her body, causing her to almost come out of the bed. Strips of paper flowed from the fetal monitor, giving the nurse an indication that she'd had another contraction.

"Hey Raven, that was a big one, huh?" Her nurse Loretta spoke softly while entering the room. Raven bonded closely with Loretta over the past few hours, well in the last day and half, as her labor began that long ago. Raven looked at Loretta as a gentle mother figure being that her own mother, Felicia, was rarely around to give love and comfort to her pregnant sixteen-year-old daughter.

"Yes, it hurt pretty bad," Raven answered. Closing her eyes, she inhaled deeply and exhaled slowly as the contraction slowly came to an end just as Loretta had instructed her to do when they'd first met.

"All the pain is worth it baby," she mumbled while gently rubbing her stomach. "In just a few hours, I will have the one thing that would make me whole."

"Yeah, it won't be long now before we get your little bundle of joy born and out into the world," Loretta smiled and gently rubbed Raven's shoulder. "Hang in there baby. You are doing great and I'm so proud of you Raven."

Raven smiled at her nurse, but the smile was quickly replaced with a frown as another contraction took over her belly and this time, her lower back was in the mix. "Oh no," she whimpered and grabbed onto the side of her hospital bed.

"Breathe," Loretta said. "Just breathe through it."

Again, Raven inhaled deeply and began to exhale but let out a growl instead. "Oh! It's hurting too bad! Please help me!"

"Okay, let me get Dr. Bass in here."

"Janice! Call Dr. Bass stat!"

"Ow, oh, ow!" Raven yelled out in pain.

"Hang on Raven, Dr. Bass is on the way."

Pain hit Raven from all different sides of her body and at different intensities.

"Stat! Get her in here stat!" Those were the last words Raven heard before everything around her changed from a heavy chaos to compete darkness.

EIGHT MONTHS EARLIER...

CHAPTER 1

Raven! I'm not going to tell you twice to come up here and wash these dishes!"

Raven rolled her eyes at the sound of her Aunt Joyce's voice. "Why do I even have to stay here?"

"Now, Raven!"

Throwing her hairbrush down on her burrowed bed, she trampled up the steps from her bedroom, which was in the basement, to the kitchen of her aunt's townhouse.

"I suggest you fix your attitude."

Ignoring her aunt, Raven continued to stomp until she made it to the kitchen sink, making a point to harshly turn the water on.

"I bet you better not break any of those dishes, girl."

Raven decided it was best to continue to keep her mouth shut; she'd learned early on that it was the best way to avoid a smack in the mouth from her mother's oldest sister. Waiting for the sink to fill with the soapy dish water, she looked outside the kitchen window and out into the back yard at the small snowflakes falling from the sky. Wintertime, specifically during the current Christmas season, was Raven's favorite time of year. In her mind, it was a chance to wish for something and maybe, just maybe, depending on what kind of mood her family was in or if her mother was taking a break from living her life selfishly, she could actually receive what she was wishing for.

"You know your mother called today."

Raven snapped out of her thoughts and turned the water off, glad that it didn't overfill. Placing the dishes in, she began to do her chore, still remaining quiet.

"I hope your momma gets herself together. Maybe she will make some New Year's resolutions to do better by her children."

"Humph, for all five of us, that would be a miracle."

"Don't you talk about yo' momma, girl! She might have her ways, but she is still you and your sister's momma. Humph, I get what you're saying through. Five girls and she can't do right by none of y'all. Don't make no sense."

Raven continued to wash the dishes while taking quick glances at the snow that was falling increasingly faster by the minute.

"Yeah. Chile, maybe your momma will get herself together one day."

Raven sighed internally and rinsed the glass that she was washing. "Yeah, maybe," she said.

"Yeah," her aunt followed. "When you get done with the dishes, I need you to run to the food store and get some more bread. You need to go ahead and go before it gets dark."

Sighing, Raven nodded her head and finished the last of the dishes. Emptying the sink and cleaning it out, just like her aunt liked it, she dried her hands, walked into the living room and smiled at the Christmas tree that loomed over the living room. An array of colorful, and boldly epic ornaments peppered with small classical angels lined the branches of the tree. Every time Raven admired the tree, she veered off into thought. Thoughts of what it would be like to have her own family and house decorated with such ornaments as her aunt did every year. Sure, her aunt was a nag, but she sure had a sense of style. Even though she'd never told her aunt how much she admired her, she did.

"Here, take this twenty instead of the five on the table. I want you to pick up some more dish liquid and flour while you're there. I told momma that I would make her some biscuits so make sure you get the self-rising kind."

"Okay."

"And get yourself something for going."

"Okay."

Grabbing her sneakers, she sat down on the chair to put them on but quickly looked out the oversized window and decided to grab her boots instead. She hated wearing the boots she had gotten for her birthday, but her grandmother bought them for her just for times like this when the snow was at its greatest. Most people in other states would lose their mind at the amount of snow that fell in Baltimore during the winter months. Unluckily and luckily for Raven, she too thought she'd lose her mind every time she was forced to go out in it by one of her family members but was lucky enough to be accustomed to it. So, going out in the snow was really no biggie for her, wasn't like she'd fall every few minutes now that she'd gotten so used to going since she'd been staying at her aunt's house. She just preferred to enjoy the warmth of the house like the ones who liked to send her out in it. Going down the stairs to her room, she pulled her boots down from the top shelf of a utility closet she turned into her closet and sat down on her bed. Slowly pulling her boots on, she stood up and stomped them down good on the floor, making sure they were nice and snug and ready for the heavy snow. Chuckling, she thought of the time she was trying to be cute when she'd first gotten her boots and fell hard on her butt and her boot went flying off of her left foot, right in front of the hottest hot boys in the neighborhood, all of them being her fellow classmates at Harriet High. Not only did she have to hide her embarrassment out in the streets, she had to hold her head up and fake laugh when someone brought it up at school.

"I definitely don't need that again," she laughed as she walked out of her bedroom and up the stairs. "Okay, auntie, I'm gone."

"Okay, be careful out there. It is really coming down."

Then why am I walking?! She quipped under her breath. *You have a car sitting right outside in the driveway. Why can't you at least take me and let me run in for you? Never mind*, she shook her head. *I don't need that drama. If I was to tell her what I was really thinking*, I would surely get a smack here and another one when we get to grandma's house, she accidently slipped the last part out of her mouth.

"Huh?"

"Huh? Oh, I didn't say anything auntie; I was singing a song," she lied.

"Okay. Well hurry up so I can go ahead and get the biscuits in the oven. Then I want you to be back before it gets dark."

"Yes ma'am," she answered before heading out the front door.

"Dang! It is cold out here!" Pulling her coat collar up around her neck, she put the money that her aunt had given her in her coat pocket and went on her way. "Agh!" She yelped as she slipped down the first two steps. "Ow! Dang, it just started snowing and it's already slippery," she hastily muttered. Slipping her hand through the top of her boot and clutching her ankle, she massaged it vigorously while holding onto the banister to collect her balance before slowly walking down the last two steps. Fully gathering her balance, she walked slowly through the accumulated snow, looking around at the other houses on the way. Mostly admiring the holiday decorations that lined most of them on her street. A few houses had Christmas trees sitting in front of the window. "That one's nice," she said aloud. The blue sparkling lights that dangled loosely on the branches caught her attention as blue is her favorite color. Slipping a bit on the sidewalk, she stopped and regathered her balance. "I got to pay attention out here," she chuckled. The snow that was falling was now a mixture of hard sleet and a bit of frozen rain. "Aw man! I know I ain't about to get stuck out here." *Then they wonder why I want a phone! Times like this when I'm sent to the store in a blizzard; a phone would be helpful.* Turning towards the direction of her aunt's house, she thought of going back but she knew her aunt would have a lot to say if she'd did that. Instead, she pulled her coat up further to cover the bottom half of her chin and worked to move a bit faster.

"Aye! Aye shawty."

Raven looked around for the face that called out to her. In the mixture of the snow and ice, it was hard to see clearly but she looked around anyway.

"Why you walking out here in this storm?"

"Who's that?" She decided to ask. It was no use to continue to try to look for the face herself. The blizzard was clouding her vision and continuing to look for the guy was wasting so much of her time.

"Come here for a sec."

Sighing, she shook her head. *I don't have time for this.* "You come here!" She called out, growing more and more frustrated by the second.

"A'ight. Hold up."

Raven smacked her lips. "Look, it's a blizzard happening right now. I'm not going to keep standing here in the—"

"Do you always have an attitude?"

Raven rolled her eyes at the boy who had walked up beside her as if nothing was going on around them. "When it's snowing like this and some boy wants me to stand out in it and wait, yes," she answered sarcastically.

"Come on. Come on my porch. Why are you even out here?"

"First of all, no, I'm not going onto your porch and secondly, I'm going to the store. Not that it's any of your business."

"A'ight baby, I was just asking. I can take you to the store. Come on my porch and let me get my keys."

"Nope, no thanks," Raven responded as she began to walk away.

"Wait, hold up. You don't want to walk all the way to the store in all this," the boy said as he lifted his hands and looked up towards the sky. "It's crazy out here."

Raven looked around at her surroundings. The blizzard like conditions had her cold, frustrated, and irritated. "Okay," she gave in. "Only because it's getting bad out here and I have to get some stuff for my aunt."

"Okay, I gotchu. Come and stand on my porch while I get my keys."

Raven stood still, not sure, if she'd made the right decision to accept a ride from a guy she didn't know.

"Come on girl! It's cold out here and I got to go work soon. Come on."

"Work?" Raven asked with a glimmer of shock and surprise. No boys she knew had jobs and they didn't want them. "Where you work at?"

The boy laughed and gently pulled Raven's hand. "I will tell you everything you want to know as soon as we get in the car and go. I'm not a deranged killer or nothing so no need to be all scared."

"I'm not scared, I just..."

"Look, my mom is friends with your aunt. Her name Joyce...right? They been friends for years."

The unnerving feeling began to disappear at the sound of her aunt's name. "Yeah," she answered and began to walk slowly to the porch.

"You got to move faster than that baby. Come on."

"I'm going as fast as I can. It's icy out here."

Chuckling, the boy held onto Raven tighter and led her to shelter, out of the icy storm. Raven held onto her companion's arm, thankful that he was around to help her out of the storm and help her to not fall flat on her face. Finally reaching the porch, she stood by the door while her friend opened it and stepped in.

"My keys are right here on the table."

Nodding her head, Raven felt a real sense of relief. Looking out at the storm, her relief transformed to gratefulness at the sight of the blistery snow and pellets of ice that fell from the sky.

"Ma! Have you seen my keys?"

Rubbing her arms, Raven looked through the window to see a warmly decorated house; an inviting look.

"Aye, come in for a minute, I got to find my keys."

"I'm good; I will wait for you out here."

"Girl, come on in, I told you that I know your aunt, so you don't have to be scared."

"I told you, I'm not scared. I just—"

"They are on the kitchen table!" A woman shouted out from the upper level of the house. "Tavon parked your truck in the garage for you!"

Grabbing Raven's arm, the guy pulled her into the house and closed the storm door slightly, leaving it ajar. "See, I will leave the door open so you can run out anytime you want."

Raven flashed a side-eye and turned her attention to the pictures that lined the walls. "Nice," she said quietly to herself.

"I'll be back ma; I'm going to go to the store real quick."

"Okay but don't you have to work?"

"Yeah but not until eight. I switched with my man so he can handle some business."

"Okay, you be careful out there. It's supposed to get worst before the night is over."

"A'ight I thought you said they were on the kitchen table. They not up there."

"Lord, boy! They probably right there in your face somewhere. You just not looking."

Raven moved closer to the door as she heard footsteps coming down the stairs.

"I told you boy; you and your brother don't use your eyes. I am always looking for—"

"Oh, hey, young lady! I didn't know we had company."

"Yeah, ma, you know her. That's Ms. Joyce's niece."

"Oh okay, yeah. How are you doing baby?"

Raven smiled, feeling more comfortable. "I'm doing good," she said shyly.

"That's good. I know Joyce has quite a few nieces. What's your name?"

"Raven."

"Okay. You have a sister named Tawanda?"

"That's my cousin; my uncle's daughter. A lot of people get her mixed up with my sister, Trina."

"Oh okay. Well, it's nice to meet you Raven."

"Nice to meet you too," Raven politely replied.

"I hate it when Tavon messes with my truck! Now I can't find my keys."

"Oh Shannon, they are in here somewhere. Your brother was just moving your truck before it started to sleet. He saw on the news that we were supposed to get some sleet and freezing rain, so he moved it to the garage for you. See, here they are, right there on the counter. You don't look for nothing!"

Raven laughed at the look on Shannon's face as he mocked his mother behind her back.

"Take the keys and go so you can come on back."

"A'ight. I'ma take..."

"Raven."

"Yeah, Raven to the store and I will be right back. Do you want me to pick up anything while I'm there?"

Raven took notice to Shannon's jet black, soft looking hair and creamy caramel complexion. *He's cute! Now that we are out of the storm, I can see how cute he is.*

"No, I just went food shopping the other day, so I think we are all good."

"A'ight. You sure you don't want a soda? I know how you like your soda."

"Nope, I already got plenty in my stash upstairs."

Shannon laughed at his mother. "I figured you did."

"Come on Raven, let's go."

Raven followed Shannon through the living room, inside the kitchen and out to the garage. Taken a back at what she saw, she figured Shannon had to be in his twenties. No teenager drove that nice of a truck around here. *Well, unless they were into something illegal.*

"It's unlocked."

Getting into the truck, Raven glanced around and admired how well-kept Shannon's truck was; how clean he kept it.

"Seatbelt."

Raven looked over at Shannon and chuckled. *Seatbelt,* she mocked.

"Yep, nobody goes anywhere without putting on their seatbelt fir—"

"I got it," Raven interrupted and quickly put on her seatbelt, smiling the entire time. Averting her attention to the opening garage door, she looked around at the snowy streets of Baltimore, admiring them and her new friend, in her eyes, her new *fine* friend, Shannon.

CHAPTER 2

You think you got problems, try staying here with grandma. Always yelling and fussing about something. And, I better not take as long as you did when she sends me to the store. I better be back in at least thirty minutes and ready to clean up and cook. Aunt Joyce said you was gone for at least two hours. Where was you at?"

Raven continued to ignore her sister, Nia, while adding more ornaments to her grandmother's tree.

"Hello!"

"I was at the store, dang. I mean it did turn into a blizzard outside," Raven responding while adding a big red ornament with white trim to the tree. "I had to walk in it. Does grandma have you all out in a blizzard?"

"Yes!" Nia laughed. "Girl, our family don't care nothing about it being a blizzard outside. To them, that's just a little bit of snow that won't kill you."

"Right," Raven replied, not really giving the conversation with her sister much thought. Instead, her mind was on Shannon. The long, slow ride to the store and back brought on a lengthy conversation about him and his family. Too embarrassed by her own family, especially her parents, Raven remained quiet for the most part and allowed Shannon to do most of talking, really only speaking when he asked her a direct question. Learning that he was a nice guy with a real job, close knit family, and having both a civilian job and holding the title of soldier in the army reserves, intrigued her. *I wonder what he's doing right now. Maybe I will call him. No, maybe I should let him call me. Maybe he already called. I should've given him grandma's number too, just in case he calls why we are over here. Ugh, I need a phone!*

"Raven?"

Raven looked at her sister and smiled. "What?" She answered shyly.

"Okay, what's his name?"

"Who?"

"Who?" Nia mocked. "The boy who got your nose wide open right now. The one... wait! Is that why you were gone so long earlier? You were with some boy when you were supposed to be at the store."

"Shhh!" Raven snapped and put the box of ornaments on the floor next to her. Walking over to the entrance to the kitchen, she listened to make sure all the adults were still deep in conversation. Hearing them laugh a few times wasn't enough, she wanted to make sure that they were too busy gossiping to pay any attention to what she and her sister were talking about.

"Whatchu doin'—?"

Raven held her finger up to stop her sister.

"Honey, she better come and get her girls. All four of them is going to be out of control if she doesn't come and take care of them herself," she heard her Aunt Anna say.

"Sure better," her grandmother joined in.

"Yep, they are talking about Ma so they will for sure be talking for hours," she muttered and walked back to the living room, sitting back down in front of the half-decorated Christmas tree.

"Alright, they still in there talking about people so tell me."

Rummaging through the ornaments, she stopped when she reached the section with the dainty little angels. "His name is Shannon and I met him when I was out walking to the store. Since it was snowing hard and started to sleet, he drove me."

"Drove?! How old is this Shannon?"

"Nia, you do know that you can get your license when you are sixteen right? You act like I'm talking about somebody in their thirties or forties," Raven chuckled.

Nia grabbed the other box of decorations and began to sort out the lights that would go on the outside of the house. "Tell me more."

"His name is Shannon."

"Yeah, I got that. What else?"

Raven looked at her sister and rolled her eyes. "He's nineteen," she continued. "He works at the post office and is in the army reserves, so he goes away on the weekends."

"Hmmm, sounds nice. So, what's good with how he looks? You said all that and ain't say nothing about him being fine or cute...something."

"Oh girl, you already know he's fine," Raven laughed. "Oh, and his hair, it's like this jet black silky soft kind of hair. I wanted to touch it but—"

"Hey, hey! My favorite nieces! How y'all doing girls?"

"Fine, how are you doing?" Raven spoke first to her uncle Charles, her grandmother's brother and the guardian of her sister, Carla.

"Hey Uncle Charles! Did you bring Carla with you?" Nia asked with a small frown on her face.

"Yeah, she's in one of her moods today," their aunt Charlotte called out while waking in the front door. "She's out in the car."

"Hi baby," she said to Raven, giving her a kiss on the cheek and then proceeded to hug and kiss Nia. "Y'all the good ones and I want y'all to stay that way."

"Yes ma'am," both Raven and Nia answered in unison.

"That girl we got staying at our house is just full of anger. I'm about to throw her out, right out there in the streets somewhere."

"Hey y'all! Y'all got it smelling good up in here!"

"Charlotte, hey girl! Come on in here and sit down!" The crowd in the kitchen greeted.

Raven was used to hearing the negative stuff about her sister but despite how she acted, she still had love for her because she was her sister. Now Nia was a totally different story. Nia didn't like Carla and Carla couldn't stand Nia. Well, she really didn't like anybody for that matter. Either they were arguing when they both got around each other or they were completely ignoring each other. Raven was different. She felt that family should always get along; should always have each other's back, no matter what. The family always said that Carla was angry because her mother was in and out of her life, a special emphasis on out, so they all just ignored her and hoped for the best.

"Why do we always have to come over here?!"

Raven watched Carla as she walked in, slammed the door, and sat down on the couch, not bothering to say a word to anyone. Looking over at Nia, Raven gave her sister the "don't do it" look before turning her attention to Carla.

"Was sup Carla?"

Carla looked at Raven as if she was the devil. "Hey," she snarled.

"Don't come up in here with all that," Nia said with attitude. "Girl don't get slapped. I will slap the—!"

"Carla, don't you want to come and help me with the decorations? I got a lot over here and I told grandma that I would have them all on the tree before dinner. You want to come and help me out?"

Carla looked at Raven, rolled her eyes, and went into their grandmother's bedroom, slamming the door hard behind her.

"Quit slamming doors lil girl!" Charlotte yelled.

Raven sighed and continued with her task of filling the tree.

"I don't even know why you bother talking to her. You know she got issues."

"Cause, she's our sister."

"Whateva, she yo' sister," Nia huffed and walked out of the living room and into the kitchen.

Raven shook her head and put the box down on the floor. Standing up, she walked over to the door and opened it. She smiled as she saw small flurries sprinkling through the dusk sky. A small group of children was running around in the yard across the street as if they had no cares. A woman joined them and began to build snowballs. Raven smiled and immediately went into thought about what it would be like to have her own children; a chance to show her mother what a real mother does for her children. "Like her," she said aloud. Looking behind her, she wanted to make sure the coast was still clear, and nobody would accuse her of talking to herself. The family was cool but very judgmental at times, especially towards *Felicia's* children. Looking back out at the family across the street, she giggled when she saw the large Golden retriever enter into the snowball fight, running around with a carefree attitude, just like the children.

Humph, I wonder what it would be like to have an actual mom like they have. Speaking of Ma, where is she? We haven't heard anything from her since Thanksgiving. Taking one last final glance at happiness, Raven closed the door and looked at the Christmas tree. The colorful lights took her mind to a happy place, a peaceful place. It was something about the brightness and the sparkle of the Christmas decorations that helped her temporarily forget about all her issues. "That one would look better on this..." she allowed her voice to trail off while moving one of the green ornaments away from another green ornament and placing it next to a red one instead. "Perfect!" She smiled.

"Does it really matter where the ornaments go Raven? What is up with the colors and all that? I mean just as long as they are up there that should be it."

"Shut up and mind yo' business."

"Whateva girl. So, that thot sister of yours finally went in hiding, huh?"

Raven looked toward her grandmother's closed bedroom door. "Yep, she's in grandma's room."

"I wish they would stop sitting in there talking about people and finish cooking so we can eat, and she can go back to Uncle Charles' house. I hate it when she comes over here."

Raven sat down on the couch and propped her feet up as thoughts of Shannon entered her mind causing her to smile. "Do you still have your phone? Didn't grandma buy you one for your birthday?"

"Girl please, she did but one of her daughters fussed her out for buying me one, so she took it," Nia replied and sat down next to Raven.

Raven laughed. "Uh, they are your aunts, not just grandma's daughters. Why are you calling them her *daughters*? Like you have no relations to them."

"Cause they act like we are just in the way; like we are not family to them. I call it like I see it."

"Hmm mmm," Raven mumbled.

"Always a way to bring me down," Raven thought quietly. "This family is wack." Again, thoughts of Shannon entered her mind; the stories he shared about his family envied her and she hated it. She wanted to be happy that Shannon's family had their lives together, but it was just hard for her to do that. *Why can't our family be like his? Why can't my sisters be like his siblings; like his brothers and his little sister. Why can't we all be close like them?* Raven smiled at the story Shannon shared about his first weekend away when he'd first became a member of the Army Reserves. *I missed them and they missed me, he'd said. When I pulled up, they were sitting on the porch, waiting for me. My mom said they had been sitting out on the porch all day that day because they wanted to be the first ones to hug me when I got back home. My little brother even slept in my bed*, she recalled Shannon's story and laughed. *I would love to have them for siblings. I don't know why I have to be stuck with the ones I have. Either they are gossiping about somebody or they are fighting and arguing with each other. Then there is his mother; a mother that I would give my right arm for; a caring mother. I don't even know*

26

where mine is most of the time. Shaking her head, hoping to shake the negative thoughts away, she turned to her sister. "I know she is not sleep... Nia?" Nia repositioned her body and slid her feet up on the couch. "Nia?" Raven chuckled and stood up. "This girl sleeps too much." Walking back to the door, she looked out towards the family that she was focused on minutes before and noticed that they'd built a snowman. "I can't wait to have a family of my own one day." Closing the door, she sighed and walked towards the kitchen, hoping that they were almost ready to eat so she could get back home and wait on a call from Shannon.

CHAPTER 3

Where is your sister? I thought she was coming over with you."

Raven glanced at her mother while walking into her home; a home that she felt should've been hers just as much it was her youngest sister but unfortunately it wasn't the case with her and her older sisters. Sure, her mother shared it with her boyfriend and his two teenaged kids, all living in the house like a one big happy family and wasn't much room to fit a cat, let alone another human being but Raven still felt that she belonged there; belonged with her mother.

"I don't know where Nia is."

"Oh, okay. What about Carla? Is she coming?"

Well, I'm here. Why are you asking about them? I'm standing here in front of you and all you can do is ask about somebody else. "I guess," she said instead of saying what was really on her mind. Raven stood by the door, waiting for her mother to fully invite her in.

"Well come on in, don't be all scared."

"I'm not scared just waiting... how are you doing Ma?" Raven felt it was in her best interest to just change the subject and not to try to school her mother on proper etiquette. Etiquette that she was taught by years of living with her aunt.

"I'm hanging in there. Taking it one day at a time, you know."

"Yeah."

There was a pregnant pause before either Raven, or her mother said a word. *Not too much to talk about when your mom is rarely around*, Raven thought internally. *I don't really know what to talk about.*

"So... how's everything going with school? You still go to Harriet, right?"

Raven held the rage inside of her the best she could. *What kind of mother doesn't know what school her child goes to?* "Yes," she answered quickly and walked over to the couch. *I guess I will just sit down. Doesn't look like she's going to ask me to sit down.*

Sitting down, she looked around her mother's house. Pictures of her younger sister were plastered all over the walls as well as other children who Raven had seen before but didn't actually know.

"You want something to drink?"

"Huh?"

Felicia laughed aloud. "Always thinking about something. What's on your mind?"

"Oh nothing, I was just looking around," she lied.

Truth be told, everything was on her mind. Mostly questions about her childhood. Questions like... *why did you decide to give me and my sisters up but decided to keep your youngest child? Why do you act like you only have one daughter instead of five?!* Raven learned long ago that she would get nothing out of her mother; no straight answers. Instead of asking, she would continue to get her information from her grandmother and her aunts whenever they got together. That was the easiest way to get the flat out, and most of the time, hurtful truth.

"Okay, do you want something to drink?"

"No, I'm good."

"Alright, if you change your mind, I have some grape soda, fruit punch, and apple juice in the fridge.

Wait, not apple juice. I have to save that for Trinity. You know how she loves her apple juice and looks for it as soon as she gets up from her nap."

Raven nodded her head and looked towards her mother's bedroom. "How is she doing?" She asked, knowing that her mother was dying to talk about her *precious* Trinity.

"Girl, my baby is doing so good! Me and her daddy just finished the last little bit of Christmas shopping for her. I was stuck in the stores because they don't have many toys that she'll want to play with. You know how your sister is; she's only five but she acts like she'll be thirty soon. All she wants to do is play with the big girl toys and her father doesn't think that she should have them. So much back and forth trying to get that girl some gifts."

"Hmmm," Raven said lightly.

"Yep, my baby is growing up on me."

Raven felt uncomfortable as she and her mother made small talk. She was never sure why but every time she spent time with her mother, she felt strange. Standing up, she walked over to the pictures and eyed each of them. "This one's new," she said while picking up the kindergarten picture of Trinity and her class.

"Yeah, they took them at the beginning of the school year this year. I just got them back a few days ago, right before the holiday break. I got to get some extras so I can give you and your sister's one."

"Right."

Raven sat back down on the couch and reverted her mind to another place, any place but at her mother's house was better. *I don't know why Grandma, Aunt Joyce, and Uncle Charles make us do this anyways. Felicia may be our mother, but she really doesn't want to be so why should we keep trying to make her be our mom? The only one she cares about is Trinity.*

"Well, I guess the other two ain't coming. Humph, I bet Momma and Charlotte got something to do with this. Make me sick!" Felicia huffed while grabbing her pack of cigarettes off the coffee table and pulling one out of the pack.

"Want one?"

Raven chuckled and shook her head. "Nope, don't smoke."

"Why not? I did when I was your age. It calms the nerves down. Here, why don't you try it? What do y'all kids say? What is it? Don't sleep on it. Ain't that what the kids are saying now? I hear Tamara and TJ say something like that all the time."

Raven looked at her mother with pure disgust mixed with borderline dislike. "No, thank you," she said as clear as she could. "I don't smoke."

"Uh, I see your ole uppity aunt got to you. I knew you was going to turn out like her. I should've sent you to stay with Momma. At least she would let you live a little. I heard you don't even have a cell phone," Felicia said before puffing some of her cigarette. "At least you would have a phone if I would've sent you to Momma's. My bad. Aye! I got that right for sure. I know for a fact that I hear my kids walking around here yelling my bad!"

"Yeah," Raven muttered an uncomfortable chuckle. "You got one," she mumbled. The doorbell snapped her out of her funk. *I hope that's Aunt Joyce. I'm ready to get out of here.*

"Speaking of that ole stuffy aunt of yours, I bet that's her at the door."

Raven remained silent as her mother got up to answer the door, being sure to take another long drag of her cigarette before she reached it.

"Hey Joyce, come on in."

"No, I'm not staying. I just came to get Raven." Joyce walked in and rolled her eyes at Felicia.

"Raven, come on; we need to get home before it starts snowing again. I don't want to get out there and get stuck."

Raven stood up, happy to be going home and leaving her mother's house. "See you later Ma," she said while walking over to the door.

"You know, you should be ashamed of yourself Felicia."

"Don't start, Joyce. This is my house and I will do what I want; when I want and there is nothing you can do about it."

"No, this is that man and his momma house. You're just staying here for a minute, but as soon as he gets tired of your sorry butt, you will be back on the streets."

"Bye, Joyce! Get on and get out of here now before I—"

"Before you what? I wish you would!"

"Why do you always come up in my house judging me? You do that all the time!"

Raven continued to stand near the door, ready to exit. *I wish Aunt Joyce would just come on!*

"All the time?! You rarely agree to see Raven so it's definitely not all the time. You are so busy chasing behind that man and his family that you forgot all about yours. You do have four girls who are out here in the world wishing that their momma was around and treated them as good as she treats her baby. It's not those girls' fault that you ain't with none of their daddies. You treat that little Trinity like she's gold all because you are still with her father...for the moment!"

"Bye Joyce! Get out!"

"As soon as he figures out that you ain't nothing, he will be throwing your behind out and you will be wanting somebody to take care of Trinity for you. Well, we are all done taking care of your kids. We are only keeping the ones you threw at us; no extras so Trinity will be on her own or—"

"I'm not going to tell you again to get out of my house! I don't have time for this!"

"Raven, it was good seeing you but y'all need to go before my man comes home and see Joyce up in here. You know he don't like her."

"Good, because I don't like him either!" Joyce spat before walking to the door.

"Raven, come on and let's get out of here!"

"Mommy."

All eyes fell on Trinity as she wiped sleep from her eyes.

"Hey baby," Felicia said tenderly and picked up her daughter, rubbing her hair while staring hastily at Raven and her sister. A single tear fell down Raven's cheek as she watched her mother become a mother in a matter of seconds; it hurt to see just how nurturing she was to Trinity. A hint of jealousy wriggled its way into the mixture of sadness and anger as she watched her mother and her little sister bond. *Why can't you hold me like that?* She thought to herself before opening the door and walking out, not saying another word.

T ook you long enough to call me. I thought
you forgot all about me."

Raven propped her feet up on the wall. "No,
I was just at my grandmother's house and we didn't get
home until late. Then I had to go and..." Raven stopped
herself, not really wanting to go through the ins and
outs about the visit with her mother. "We stay at my
grandmother's house late sometimes."

"Oh, dat's was sup."

At the sound of Shannon's voice, Raven blushed
like she's never blushed before. Although she thought
he was cute and all when she'd first met him, she didn't
have this much of a reaction until the conversation with
her sister, Nia, at her grandmother's house. Now she
was sure it was more than a small crush.

"Whatchu doing right now?"

Raven shifted her weight on her bed and looked over at the basement walls. "Nothing, just chillin'."

"Come outside then."

Raven sat up on her bed. Immediately thinking of an excuse to get out of the house and out of her aunt's grip. Not coming up with anything, she sighed. "My aunt don't like me going out when it's getting dark out. She's kind of old fashioned and think that I should be in the house before the streetlights come on."

Shannon laughed and Raven's stomach dropped due to the immense feeling of embarrassment. Instead of giving in to her feelings, she did the only thing that she knew how to do in this situation, become full of attitude.

"What?!" She blurted out as mean as possible.

"Yo, chill baby. I wasn't laughing at you. I was laughing because my mother is the same way."

Raven put her hand over her mouth to keep herself from blurting out any more embarrassing statements. "My bad," she said quickly. *He's going to think I'm crazy if I don't chill.*

"It's all good. Well, if you can't come out right now, then we will link up another day. I'm off all day tomorrow if you want to chill then."

40

"A'ight," she said quickly. Perhaps, a little too quickly.

"A'ight."

The phone conversation grew silent for a minute. *What do I say now? I wish Nia was here; she would know what to say.*

"So, you got any plans for Christmas?" *Christmas, that's safe to talk about.* "I'm supposed to go over to my grandmother's house and chill with my sisters."

"Oh word. How many sisters do you have?"

"Four," she said slowly. The mention of the number of sisters she had kind of embarrassed her. Mainly because her entire family always judged her mother for having five children and only took care of one of them. The fact that her family had an opinion caused havoc on her; she always thought people were ready to judge her because of her mother's decisions.

"Oh, dat's was sup. You got four extra girls to jump on somebody if needed huh?"

Raven laughed, grateful that she wasn't being judged. Beginning to open up a little more, she began to speak about her sisters. "Well, just three. My youngest sister is five so she can't do nothing."

Shannon laughed and Raven's heart melted.

"I'm closest with my sister, Nia, so she would be the one to jump on somebody."

Raven and Shannon both laughed at the same time.

"Okay, I feel you. You know that I have a younger sister and two younger brothers. Me and my brother, Tavon, is only a year a part. The two little ones are a year a part, seven and eight."

"Oh wow."

"Yeah, my parents started all over again, as they both say."

"Yes, they did," Raven laughed.

"So, you go to school? Tell me more about yourself."

"Like what?"

Shannon laughed. "Like stuff about you. You know, stuff like school and stuff that you like to do."

Here it is, Raven muttered under her breath. *Well, he seems to be pretty cool so I can tell him about my life...just a little, I guess.* "Yep, I go to Harriet High."

"Yeah, my cousin went there a few years ago. I heard it was lit up in there."

"Lit?" Raven laughed. "More like lame."

"Of course, you will think it's lame; you go there. Everybody thinks their school is lame. I went to Eastern Tech, so I don't know too much about Harriet."

"You went to the school that all the nerds... I mean, smart people go."

"Ha! Did you just try to play me?"

"No," Raven laughed. "I didn't mean to say that."

"Yeah right."

"I swear I wasn't tryin' to play you," Raven laughed harder.

"Whateva, it's all good though."

The phone chatter once again grew silent. Thinking hard on other stuff to talk about, Raven's mind went into overdrive. *I wish I had more experience with boys! I would know what to talk about if I had.*

"Raven, you need to get out more," she heard Nia's voice.

Hmmm, now I know why Nia always says that. I would have so much more to talk about had I did what she told me to do. Think Raven...think!

"So, um, what does your mom do?" *Ugh, really Raven?* She scolded herself. *Who asks about somebody's mother right away? Out of all the questions I could've asked.*

"My mom is a nurse; works mostly during the day when my little brother and sister are at school. Yeah, my mom, that's my girl. I'd do anything for my mom. She's my heart."

Raven nodded her head; the only thing she knew to do. In fact, anytime she came across someone who was close with their mom, she would nod her head and keep her mouth shut. *Wish I can say the same.* "That's sweet." Looking over at the washing machine, she sighed internally, *I can't wait to get out of here and get my own place. At sixteen, that would be impossible.*

"Then my dad is a truck driver."

Raven snapped out of her entrance to her daydream of leaving her aunt's house and being out on her own at the sound of Shannon's voice.

"Oh, that's was sup," she said.

"Yeah, He's rarely home but I hold it down while he's gone. At least when I'm not doing one of my weekends with the Reserves."

"Yeah, I remember you saying something about that the other day. What do you actually do?"

"Yeah, it's a branch of the Army. Soldiers go away one weekend out of each month for duty and then we stay home the rest of the month."

Soldier, that sounds so good.

"Yep, I spend my time doing stuff. Try to be a good example for my little sister and brothers, you know?"

"Yeah, dat's was sup. That's cool... you know...being a soldier and all."

"Well my dad was in the Army for twenty years; just retired not that long ago. So, I wanted to follow in his footsteps."

"Oh ok. So, your dad was in the Army Reserves too?"

"No, he was in the Army. I chose the Reserves so I could go to college all while I'm serving. I start classes in January."

"Wow, you seem like you got all your stuff together. What are you going to college for?"

"I want to be a detective so I'm going to take my prerequisites so that I can go into the police academy. I really don't have to do all that, but the Army is paying so I figured I would go and get all the education I can get."

"Right," Raven chuckled. "If I had it like that, I would do the same. I want to go to college, but I don't think I will be able to."

"Why not?"

"Because, I don't have any money to pay for it. It cost so much just to go to the community college around here."

"Well you know you can get financial aid; TPU has a lot of programs that you can take advantage of. You know, there are a lot of programs that help people pay for college."

I can't believe this. A boy who is into college, making money the right way, in the Army, and doing good in life. Not like all the other boys I know; trying to play like they hard. Hanging out on the corner all day calling themselves slinging. They ain't about nothing. Here is a boy who ain't about all that. Finally!

"You should look into TPU. That's where I'm going."

"Okay, I will," Raven smiled.

"A'ight, so, we talked all about me and my people. Was sup with yours? You have four sisters, you live with your aunt, you fine, and you go to Harriet. So, what else is there to know about you?"

Did he just say I was fine? Her stomach flipped in a bunch of excited and nervous knots, all at the same exact time, giving her a bit of a stomachache. Her smile was so big that she thought her head was going to explode from the pain that was coming from her cheeks. *Okay Raven, don't say the wrong stuff and turn him away. Keep Ma out of the conversation as much as possible.* "Uh, well, I really don't have anything else to say about myself." Shifting herself on her bed, she thought carefully on what to share. Looking over at the washing machine, she looked towards the stairs and then back at the machine. *I hope Aunt Joyce don't come down here right now to finish the laundry. I don't want her to open her big mouth and spill the beans that I'm from a crazy family with loud mouths. That would for sure push him away before I can even tell him more about myself.*

"Yes, you do. Everybody has stuff to share about themselves. Was sup? Do you have any girls you roll wit'?"

"Nah, not really. Just my sisters and a few girls from school when I'm there. We really don't do nothing outside of school."

"Yeah, I feel you."

"What about your mom? Was sup with you staying with your aunt? Your father?"

Oh boy, here it goes. "Well, my dad decided to dip when I was three months old and my mom had a lot going on in life, so my aunt brought me home to stay with her when I was around five."

"Damn, that's messed up. I can't see myself just walking out of my kid's life like that. What about your mom? Like do y'all talk and stuff?"

There was a pause before the conversation continued. Raven normally felt extremely uncomfortable but for some reason, talking to Shannon, she felt the most comfortable telling him about what she named, the "deadbeats" that were her parents.

"Yeah, I see her from time to time."

"Well at least you talk to her sometimes."

There was another brief pause before Raven spoke. "Yeah," she answered lightly. Looking back over to the washing machine, the light beamed for the rinse cycle. *I don't want her to come down here...not now.*

"Hold on for a minute." Raven put the phone down and walked to the stairs.

"Aunt Joyce! I got the clothes! I will put them in the dryer!"

"Huh?!"

Raven lifted her head, looked towards the ceiling, back at the phone that was lying on her bed, and back at the entrance of the stairs. "I will put the clothes in the dryer for you!" She yelled louder.

"Okay! Thanks baby!"

"You're welcome!"

Flopping back down on her bed, she smiled and picked up the phone. "I'm back. So, do you work tonight?" Feeling more confident and relieved at the fact that her "normal family" cover wouldn't be blown, at least for the moment, she crossed her legs and waited for the conversation to continue.

"No, I'm off tonight. My mom said it was supposed to snow again so I'm glad I don't have to go in."

"Yeah," Raven said and hopped back off her bed. Walking over to the washing machine, she turned the end of cycle buzzer off, pulled the clothes out with her free hand, and quickly threw them into the dryer. "Hmm hmm, it does look like it's about to snow."

"Yep."

"Huh?!"

Raven listened while Shannon spoke to someone in the background.

"Okay! I gotchu'."

"Aye, I'ma hit you back in a little while. I got to help my mom with something real quick."

"Okay."

Hanging up the phone, Raven felt a sense of glee; she felt more alive than she had ever felt before. "I need to call Nia!" Turning to lay flat on her stomach, she dialed her sister's cell phone, glad that their grandmother decided to give it back to her and waited for her to answer. "I wish I can get a phone, that's all I'm missing," she sighed, as she was ready to burst out of her skin, aching to tell her sister all about her phone call with the one and only, Shannon.

CHAPTER 5

C hile, if you don't come on, we are going to be late getting everything ready before the family gets here."

Raven smiled and remained silent. *Not even you can ruin my mood today, Aunt Joyce. I am so happy right now.* Moving the broom but not really sweeping anything, she thought of her chat with Shannon. *One of the good ones; I can't let him get away.*

"Raven, make sure you go and get the gifts for Momma and 'em off my bed. I want to put them under the tree before they get here."

"Yes ma'am." Stopping for a second, she admired the Christmas tree one last time before Christmas. Yes, her aunt was blissfully in the holiday spirit, but the tree was always quickly taken down the day after Christmas. Sometimes, she would get the family together right after they all exchanged gifts to help take it down on Christmas day. Walking up the stairs, she glanced at the pictures on the wall and smiled at one when she was a baby. A welcomed change to what she sees at her mother's house; or lack of. She never saw any pictures of her and her sisters. Nobody except for her mother's favorite. Yes, a welcomed switch; somebody actually cared enough about her to put up some pictures of her and make her feel like she was home and had a home. Opening the door to her aunt's bedroom, she surveyed the array of colors lying on the bed. Presents of all sizes sprawled all over, some spilling onto the floor. Smiling, she walked over closer and sat down. Grabbing the first gift, she looked for the nametag and hoped that it was hers. *Maybe it's a phone in one of these.* Pulling on the tag, she tossed it over on the side when she saw *Momma* written on it. Searching for the smaller ones, she pulled one that was small; small enough to hold some socks but too big for shoes. "The perfect size for a phone!" She muttered. Shaking the box, she smiled gleefully and placed it off to the side by itself, making sure that would be the first one she opens once it was her turn to open some of her gifts.

"Raven! Momma and 'em are on the way. Come on and bring the presents down! And you better not be trying to shake them to find out if you can figure out what you got!"

Raven giggled and grabbed the basket on the other side of her aunt's bed, replacing the clothes with the wrapped items. "I really hope it's a phone in one of these." Quickly running down the stairs, she placed the gifts one by one under the tree, putting the one with her name on it in the front.

"You took long enough, chile."

"Sorry Auntie, I was just making sure I got them all." She sat down on the chair next to her aunt and admired the tree.

"So, what are you looking forward to getting this year for Christmas?"

A huge smile formed on her face as she thought of the exact phone that she hoped was in one of those boxes.

"Let me guess, a phone. Is that right?"

Raven was excited to see her aunt smiling for a change. Maybe it was the Christmas cheer that had her in a good mood but whatever it was, it was working in Raven's favor. "Yes!" She exclaimed excitedly. "Auntie, you know I always wanted a phone and I really want one bad this year."

"Uh huh, why do you want a phone so bad? We have a phone here at the house. Why do you need an extra phone?"

Raven thought quickly; she had to make sure she said the right thing. It was no way her aunt would come out of her old-fashioned ways and be comfortable with her having a phone if all she wanted to do was call and text Shannon all day. Whenever, wherever, and how often she wanted to. "I just want to be able to call you from school if I have to."

"School? They have phones at—"

"And... I want to be able to have a way to call you when I walk to the store to make sure that I am getting everything you need. You never know, you may need something that you forgot to tell me about. If I had a phone, you could just call me, and I can get what it is you forgot to tell me about." *Ding, Ding! That got her,* Raven cheered as she seen her aunt's face slowly make way for a smile.

"Yeah, you got a point there. Well, we will see, chile. Let's get in the kitchen, get the rest of the food, and stuff out on the table. Momma and 'em will be here soon."

Following her aunt into the kitchen, Raven happily opened the fridge to help prepare the table.

"Oh shoot! Raven, I might have to send you to the store. We forgot to get the paper plates and the paper cups."

Raven looked over at the big pack of plates and cups that had been sitting there for weeks.

"Uh, okay auntie." Grabbing the bowl of gravy, Raven sat it on the counter next to the stove. Her aunt taught her a little about cooking when she'd first taken her in; just the basics. Nothing too fancy like collards or turkey but she did teach her how to fry fish and make the best tartar sauce to go with it. Homemade gravy, *Sock-it-to-me Gravy*, the name her aunts and grandmother gave it, was the next thing she was taught. Along with when to reheat before the family came over to eat it.

"You know we have to have the colorful holiday edition cups and plates. Can't use the ones we have on the table."

Why not? Raven huffed to herself. *It all does the same thing; drink from and eat off of.* "Right," she said instead and sat down next to her aunt.

"Make sure you try to hurry. You know Momma and 'em will be here soon and they are going to want to eat!"

Raven laughed along with her aunt. "Yes ma'am. I will. At least it's not snowing. I should be able to get there quickly." Nice black hair and a gorgeous smile entered into her mind first, followed by his voice; *Shannon,* she said mentally and smiled. *Maybe I will run into him. Maybe I should go and knock on his... Too much Raven,* she chuckled. *I will not go and knock on his door. I ain't thirsty like that.* Smiling, she looked over at the window while waiting for her aunt to find her money; money that she always loses within her overly crowded purse.

"Where did I put that twenty-dollar bill? I got to clean this bag out."

"Yes, you do," Raven laughed.

"Hush," Joyce laughed and playfully smacked Raven on the thigh while rumbling through her bag. "Here it is! Lord, take me forever to find this money.

Momma will be here before you can even get out to the store."

Getting her coat off the coat rack, Raven slipped it on quickly and grabbed her scarf. Thoughts of Shannon crowded her mind, which caused her to move faster. *I hope he sees me. Please let him see me.*

"Go ahead so we can get this dinner going. I will do the gravy while you're gone."

"Yes ma'am."

"Okay and be careful out there. Ilene fell today trying to walk faster than she can. Just had that surgery not too long ago; I don't know why them girls had her walking out there in the first place."

Raven shook her head at her aunt and her rants while she walked into the kitchen. Walking out on the front porch, she looked down on the steps to survey them. "Not too bad and it's not too cold out here." Starting her journey, she started slowly to avoid icy spots but moved a little faster than normal to get to Shannon's house as fast as she could.

"Hey Raven!"

Raven looked towards the street and waved at two of her classmates.

"Was sup y'all!" She said and continued to walk.

Walking by, she slowed her footsteps and looked over at his house. *Yes, the door is open. Maybe he will see me walking by and come outside. Just go over there and knock on the door. Stopping by does not make you thirsty,* her inner voice whispered to her. *Just do it,* it continued. Stopping, she put her head down as the nerves in her stomach were flipping around so hard that it began to hurt. *Just go Raven.* Huffing, she walked slowly towards his door but quickly turned around. *Nope,* she quipped. *If he sees me, then he just sees me. If not, then I will see him later.*

"Looking for me?"

Raven looked towards the sound of the voice that made her feel all giddy and anxious all at the same time, every time she heard it.

"No," she smiled. "It looks like you were looking for me," she said with an unfamiliar boost of confidence.

"Yeah right. You were looking for me. Don't even try to play me like that."

"Whateva."

"Going to the store?"

"Yep."

"Come on, I'll take you."

"Nah, I'm good. It's not snowing so I can walk."

"You can walk even if it is snowing but you know you want a ride, so come on. You know I gotchu."

Raven turned towards the street and blushed like she was the main chick in an Instagram video and all eyes were on her. Making sure Shannon didn't see her smiling all hard, she kept her face and her eyes towards the street, looking at nothing. "A'ight," she said quickly and walked over towards him, working hard to lessen her smile.

"That's what I thought. You know you like riding in my truck, so stop playn'."

Raven laughed and walked to his car, waiting for him to unlock the door.

"Go ahead and get in."

"Uh, it's locked," she said with a hint of attitude, just enough to throw him off at the fact that she liked him and liked him a lot.

"Oh, my bad. Hold up."

Raven watched Shannon as he walked into his house. "Yesss!" she happily cried out. I am so glad Aunt Joyce needed something from the store!"

"Hey dear. How are you doing today?" Shannon's mother called out from the open kitchen door that led to the garage.

"Hi," Raven smiled and waved hello. "I'm fine. How are you doing today?"

"I'm doing good baby. Thanks for asking. Are you all ready for Christmas?"

Why can't my mom be like that? "Yes ma'am," she answered with a smile.

"I know your aunt is cooking. She sure can cook!"

"Yes ma'am," Raven chuckled. We are having dinner with the family tonight at our house."

"Oh, I see. Well, you enjoy and if I don't see you anymore before Christmas, you have a good one and be sure to remember the real meaning of Christmas."

"Yes ma'am," Raven replied.

"Go ahead and get in, I just unlocked it."

"See you later!" Raven called out to Shannon's mom before hopping into the truck.

Gosh, I wish my mom was like that. He has a good mother. Looking around in the car, she smiled. *It would be nice to have a ride like this. Shannon has it all.*

"A'ight, put that seat belt on and let's ride."

Raven smiled and clicked her seat belt into place. Leaning back, she looked out the window as Shannon drove out of his driveway and onto the street. Light snow began to fall and Raven chuckled. "I'm so glad you are taking me. I don't feel like having snow smack me all in my face."

"Yeah, it's been snowing a lot around here. I will be glad when it stops."

"Yeah, me too."

Stopping at the light, Shannon relaxed his grip on the steering wheel and looked over at Raven.

Beginning to feel the heat rise in the pit of her stomach, she turned slightly to her right, hoping that it would shield her from his stare.

"You turning the other way ain't gonna stop me from looking at you."

Raven giggled slightly and shook her head. "Why are you staring at me?" She continued to look out the window while waiting for his answer; watching the trees and the sidewalks whip past.

"I like looking at pretty girls."

Oh no, now I'm sure to get a headache from smiling so hard. "Thanks," she managed to get out with a straight face before turning back towards the window.

"What is everybody out here trying to get?"

Raven looked at the entrance to the store and sighed. "It's been crowded over here lately. I wish they would all just go home or go to another store. This is not the only grocery store around here."

"Yeah, but I guess it's the closest for people to get here in our neighborhood."

Raven shook her head and waited for Shannon to find a parking space. "Good luck with finding somewhere to park."

"Ain't nowhere to park at all over here," Shannon laughed. Just run in real quick and I will sit right here."

"Uh, it's illegal to park in a load—"

"Yes, mom, I know."

Raven laughed and got out of the truck, rolling her eyes at Shannon before she went into the store. Shannon blew a kiss at her and Raven thought she was going to pass out. Raven walked as quickly as possible so that she could hurry and get back in the truck with Shannon. Every time she was with him or talked to him on the phone, she felt as if she was the only girl in the world.

"Excuse me suga'," an elderly lady walked past, nearly knocking Raven down. Raven moved over slightly to allow the woman to pass and then she rushed to the section with the paper plates and paper cups. "They don't have any red ones. I should've known they were going to be out of that type of stuff." Sighing, she searched the aisle for something festive enough to please her aunt. "Those should work," she mumbled while pulling down a pack of green cups and some plates with pictures of leaves on the edges of them. "These will have to do." Rushing to the self-checkout counter, she waited in line behind a man with two small children. *They need to open some more registers in here. Always got workers staring people down but won't open a register. They are so wack up in here.* Raven waited impatiently while the man in front of her tried to figure out how to ring up some bell peppers. Smacking her lips, she turned and looked around in the store, hoping that her gazing would help her take her mind off the crowds in the store and the chaos at the self-checkout section. "Damn," she sighed as she watched the man press the help button. *Now we have to sit and wait for somebody to come over here.* The slight whimper of the baby in the car seat took Raven's mind off her frustration. A small baby boy lay snug in his car seat while a little girl, probably around three stood next to the man, no doubt was her father because she looked just like him. Smiling, she looked closer into the cart at the car seat, hoping to see the baby. A full-blown cry escaped the baby's lips and Raven's heart lit up. "Awww, a newborn baby."

"Daddy! The baby is crying!"

"Yes, I hear him, sweetie."

"Daddy!"

"Olivia, hang on baby."

Raven smiled at the little girl and Olivia smiled back.

"Hi," she said shyly.

"Hi," Raven spoke softly.

"My baby brother is crying."

"Aww, I know."

"His name is Sam."

Raven giggled. "Okay, that's a nice name."

"Yeah, he's crying."

"Yeah," Raven replied and began to loosen up.

"My name is Olivia."

"Hi Olivia, it's nice to meet you."

"Yeah, Sam is crying," Olivia repeated.

Raven smiled and repositioned her items in her hands. "I see," she said and chuckled.

"Olivia, get Sam's pacifier out of his bag for me please."

Raven watched as Olivia worked hard to find Sam's pacifier. She listened as Sam's cries gotten louder.

"I can't find it, Daddy."

"I can help," Raven said quickly.

"Oh, thanks so much," the man said. "I really appreciate that."

"No problem."

"Uh, excuse me! I need some help with this!"

"Sure," one of the employees finally rushed over to offer her assistance.

Raven smiled at Olivia once again as she looked through Sam's bag. Placing her items on the counter, she turned back to Sam's bag as his crying turned to tiny whimpers. The smell of baby powder brightened her eyes as she pulled the pacifier out. Reaching into the cart and into the car seat, Raven thought she would die of happiness. It was something about the baby that caused her heart to melt and face to brighten up. "He is adorable," she whispered to herself. Putting the pacifier in Sam's mouth, she thought of what it would be like to have her own baby. "Hi Sam," she cooed. Sam looked at her and closed his eyes. "Aww, he's so sweet." Raven touched Sam's hand and he grabbed onto her finger and squeezed. His little small fingers felt like silk in Raven's hand. *I know I will be a better mother than mine has ever been.*

"Thank you, young lady. I really appreciate your help."

"Oh, uh, you're welcome." Raven let go of the baby's hand and picked her items up off the counter. Time moved quickly as Raven attended to the baby.

"Bye," Olivia said to Raven as she walked towards the exit with her father.

"Bye," Raven replied before she scanned the cups. *I want a baby*, she said to herself as she scanned the plates. *Yes, a baby to love will solve all my problems. I can show my mom how to be a good mom with my own baby.* Putting the money in the machine, she waited for her change and the receipt. Thinking of Sam and the smell of baby powder, she smiled. *Yep, a baby is all I need. I will have somebody to love and he or she would love me back. Then maybe, my mom will want to be my mother once I teach her how to be one.*

Grabbing her change and the receipt, Raven walked out of the store with a new purpose for her life, to be a mom.

CHAPTER 6

C hristmas! It's finally here," Raven whispered as she opened her eyes. Looking around in the basement, she stretched her arms up as high as she could and sat up in her bed. The musty smell of the basement wasn't going to get her down today because the day had finally arrived that she had been waiting on for months. The medium sized gift that she found on her aunt's bed with her name on it had her mind and she was eager to finally get to it. Hopping out of bed, she slipped her feet into her slippers and rushed upstairs to the living room. The lights on the tree still glistened brightly from the night before. All the presents were scattered under the tree, giving Raven a new burst of energy

"You finally up, huh?"

"Merry Christmas, Aunt Joyce."

"Merry Christmas, baby. Go on and open your gifts. I know you were so ready to get to them."

Raven smiled and sat on the floor near the tree. Shreds of tinsel fell onto Raven's hair as she searched for the girt that had her mind in a state of excitement.

"I think you should open that big one over there in the back first," Aunt Joyce said while sipping on her coffee.

Ugh, no, not that one, she screamed internally. The one that might be a new phone. "Okay," she replied and pulled the box towards her.

"That's from your grandmother."

Opening the box, she found two pairs of ripped skinny jeans and two shirts to match.

"That's so nice, Raven and you really needed some new clothes."

"Yes ma'am, it's nice. I will call Grandma and thank her for them." Finally spotting the gift that she was looking for, she scooped it up and began removing the wrapping paper. The tip of the box was pink, and Raven thought she was going to break her face from smiling so hard. Pulling the rest of the paper off, she laughed aloud and looked over at her aunt, who was smiling at her.

"I know you wanted one for quite some time and you do need one."

Raven opened the box and pulled her brand-new phone out. "Thanks so much, Aunt Joyce!" She squealed.

"You're welcome baby. That's a fancy one; you got to show me how to work it. The girl at the store said it was one of the light phones out."

Raven laughed hard. It's *lit*, Aunt Joyce.

"Oh, what I say?"

"You said light," Raven said through her laughter.

"Oh, well, whatever it's called. The girl said you would like that one."

Raven smiled as she ran her hands over the glass that covered the phone. *Now, I can finally FaceTime Nia and not be the only one in school without a phone. Yes!*

"It's a case over there somewhere. The girl said you should go ahead and put the case on because the phone is made up of glass."

"Yeah, it is," Raven smiled and poked through the rest of her gifts. Seeing a few from her other aunts, she searched for the one with Aunt Joyce's name on it;

anxious to get to the case. "I will open the other ones after I put my case on. I do not want to break this! OMG! I am so happy right now!"

"Good, I'm glad you like it," Aunt Joyce said before she sipped more of her coffee and walked over to the door. "It's starting to snow again."

Raven looked out the door and smiled. Thoughts of Shannon filled the spaces in her mind as she looked out. *I can call Shannon with my own phone. Yes!* Getting up off the floor, Raven closed her eyes in excitement and opened them back up quickly. *I got to get his number.* Picking up the phone, she searched to open the call list.

"Who you calling this early? Your sister?"

"Nah, I need to get my friend's number off the phone. I want to add it to my phone. And then I need to get Grandma's number so I can add it to my contacts."

"Okay, girl. Go on with your phone business. I'm going to go and get ready so we can go over to Momma's house."

"Okay."

Raven searched the contact list for Shannon's cell number. *I think this is it. 443,* she read silently to herself. *443- 867,* she continued to recite while adding the numbers to her contacts. *S-h-a-n-n-o-n*, she typed in. Next, she typed in her grandmother's number, followed by Nia's. Going back to Shannon's number, she smiled as she added heart emoji's next to his name. She went back to her grandmother's name and added an angel emoji next to hers. Then she went back to her sister's name and stared at it. "What do I add for Nia...?" Searching the array of emoji's and stickers, she laughed when she came across an angry looking one. "Yeah, since she always mad at somebody." Adding the emoji, she smiled and thought of her other sisters. "I don't need their numbers," she mumbled.

What are you... no, erasing the message, she typed in *wyd* instead.

Who dis...?

Raven laughed loudly and sat up higher on the couch.

Me.

In a matter of minutes, Raven's phone rang loudly, startling her. The angry looking emoji stared back at her next to Nia's name. *How does she even know I got a phone and how does she have the number?*

"Heyyy," Raven smiled as she greeted her sister.

"Raven! Was sup girl! You finally got your phone."

"Yep. How did you know—?"

"Girl, I'm the one who convinced Aunt Joyce and grandma to let you have the phone. Aunt Joyce gave me the number as soon as she got it."

Raven giggled, "I should've known you were behind all this."

"Yep, you know I got yo' back."

"Yeah," Raven smiled. "Whatchu doing?"

"Nothing, just sitting here. Getting ready to grease grandma's scalp so she can put her big white church hat on that she was saving just for this day."

Raven laughed and walked over to the door. Big snowflakes fell hard to the ground, covering the old snow with a fresh coat.

"What is Aunt Joyce up to?"

"She's upstairs getting ready so we can come over there. Probably looking for her big church hat."

The sisters laughed in unison and continued small talk about family, friends, school, and Christmas gifts.

"Okay girl let me link up with Daryl. I need to tell him "Merry Christmas" before his sensitive butt think I don't care about him."

Raven laughed. "You need to leave that boy alone."

Nia followed Raven in laughter. "Girl, you right but don't nobody else want him so I got to stay with him."

"Bye Nia! I will see you later today."

"Okay girl. I will help you program your phone when you come over."

"It seems like it's already programmed. You know how Aunt Joyce is. I think she got the people at the phone store to do all that. Everything seems to be working on it."

"Oh okay, maybe she did. I can still look at though."

"A'ight."

Raven hung up the phone and immediately thought of Shannon.

"Here is the song right here!"

Raven smiled at her aunt while she danced to Donny Hathaway's, *This Christmas* as she placed a big pan of cinnamon rolls into the oven.

"This Christmas!" Joyce shouted.

Raven laughed and looked down at her phone. Quickly hitting Shannon's name, she hit the text button.

Hey...

Erasing that, she smiled and typed in...

Merry Xmas

Staring at her phone, a barrage of butterflies had overtaken her stomach. She gasped when she saw *typing* display on her phone.

Merry Xmas... wat up

Feeling full of glee mixed with a bundle of anxious nerves, she quickly typed into her phone.

Chillin'

"Raven, go ahead and start getting dressed. We going to go ahead and head over to momma's after the cinnamon rolls get ready."

"Okay," she replied and smiled at the *Typing* signal that once again popped up on the screen.

A'ight. Stop by my house before you go to your gma house.

Raven's heart skipped two beats. *How does he know it's me?* The butterflies in her stomach began to swarm faster as she thought of a second reason why he would reply the way he did. *Maybe he thinks I'm some other girl that he is talking to.* Reading the text message again, she began to type, but stopped. Looking at the audio button, she contemplated pushing it but swiftly changed her mind. Sadness gripped her but before she could react, a new message appeared.

Raven...

Feeling a huge sense of relief and happiness, she responded to Shannon's message.

Yep...

A silly faced emoji followed her message and she laughed. *I guess he don't play with girl's feelings. Maybe I am the only girl he talks to. I mean, how else would he know it was me and I just got this phone?*

I will stop by.

Raven waited for a response, but nothing happened. The best Christmas ever! She said before heading down to the basement to grab something cute to wear... just for Shannon.

"Thanks for the clothes Grandma! I love them!"

"You're welcome Raven. You need some new clothes and that's so much better than toys."

Raven and Nia looked at each other and snickered.

"Grandma, we don't play with toys anymore," Nia said through giggles.

"Well, y'all should. Y'all getting too grown."

"Yeah, we know," Nia said to her grandmother and kissed her on the cheek.

"Come on, Raven, let's go in my room."

Raven followed her sister up the stairs and to her room, speaking and waving at family who gathered every Christmas to have dinner at her grandmother's. "The House," as all her family called it, was packed with family and friends from all over. Walking into her sister's room, Raven felt a twinge of jealousy. Although she didn't want to be jealous of her sister, she was, every time she went into her bedroom. *Why does Nia get to get a regular bedroom and I'm stuck sleeping in an ole musty ass basement?* That question always came to mind when she was sitting in Nia's room.

"Let me see that phone, chick."

Snapping out of her storm of envy, she pulled her phone out of her jacket pocket and handed it to Nia.

"Nice." Nia said as she inspected it. "This was sup, Raven."

Raven looked at her sister and nodded her head before gazing around at the bright purple walls with splashes of colors decorated over top of the purple to match. "I like your new paint. When did you get that done?"

"Oh, Grandma called one of the deacons from church to do it. Grandma saw something at his house painted like that, so she asked him to come over and paint mine. It looks crazy, but you know how Grandma is. What she says goes."

"I like it," Raven complimented and hopped onto Nia's daybed.

"Ugh, why? It looks like somebody just took a bunch of paint and threw it on the walls," Nia laughed.

"Right! That's what makes it nice."

"Whateva. Did you...wait...Shannon? I see you wasted no time adding Shannon to your contacts and with hearts!"

Raven stood up and snatched her phone out of her sister's hand. "Mind yo' business," she laughed.

"You don't have nobody else up in your phone but me, Grandma, and Shannon. Where all the other people at?"

"They cool; I just haven't added them yet."

"Right but you got around to adding Shannon."

"So!" Raven snapped. The smile on her face told it all but she continued to try to act like it was no big deal that Shannon was the first and only person, outside of her family, that had a spot in her phone.

"Defensive...check! That big ole Kool-Aid smile on your face... check! The—"

"Okay, a'ight. I like him, dang!" Raven threw a teddy bear at her sister and laughed.

"I know you do. Call him so I can talk to him."

"What?! No, I'm not calling him so you can talk to him."

"Why not? I need to feel him out. Make sure he ain't bad for you and all that stuff. You know, do my sisterly duty."

Raven shook her head and put her phone in her pocket. "No thanks, I know he's cool. I don't need your help."

"I didn't say that you needed my help. I know you can take care of yourself, but I need to do my part too. You know take on—"

"I don't need you to do nothing for me!"

Raven and Nia both stopped and looked over at the door.

"Is that Ma?" Raven asked with a frown etched across her face.

"Sounds like it." Nia mumbled.

"Look Joyce, you don't tell me that I can't come and see my momma on Christmas! I can come over here anytime I want."

"Yep, that's her," Nia said and rolled her eyes. "Why is she even here right now? Making all that noise."

Raven remained quiet. She was happy that her mother had decided to come over and join the family. She always held a glimmer of hope that her mother would do better by her family, especially by her daughters. "Let's go and see her," Raven suggested slowly, not sure how her sister would take that.

"Shannon must really got you messed up cause you trippin' now. You know I am not going down there and blessing her with my presence."

Raven thought of Shannon and the relationship he'd had with his mom and it pushed her to want the same type of relationship with her mother. "I'll be right back." Raven walked out of her sister's room as fast as she could; hoping that she wouldn't follow her downstairs and make an even bigger scene.

"Felicia, just go somewhere and sit down."

81

"You better go and sit down somewhere! As a matter of fact, go and have several seats before I knock you out!"

"Really Ma?" Raven mumbled while hesitantly walking down the stairs.

"Oh, chile please! You ain't gonna smack nobody over here!"

Raven huffed at the sound of her aunt Joyce's and her mother's voices going back and forth at each other.

"Mommy!" Raven yelled as loud as she could; hoping that would get her mother's attention.

"That's your problem, Joyce. You think just because you got one of my daughters staying with you, that you can tell me what to do. "Hey, Raven. How you doing?"

"Fine. Why are you yelling, Ma?"

"Oh, don't you start with me girl! I came here to see Momma. I didn't come here to fuss with your aunts or to answer questions from you!"

Raven crossed her arms and shook her head.

"Where my baby at? I got to get out of here! That's why I don't like coming here!"

"Trinity! Let's go! Go get in the car with Daddy."

"You really need to get yourself together, Felicia. You are just a mess and you need to get it together."

Raven watched in disbelief as her mother walked over to her aunt and pushed her.

"Felicia, go somewhere with that. I'm—"

"Hey! Y'all stop with that mess!"

Now they got Grandma all pissed off. Raven stood in the corner of her grandmother's kitchen and silently watched the fiasco go down with her aunt and her mother.

"Mommy!" Trinity screamed right before Joyce pushed her mother into the wall.

"Oh, it's on now," Raven said aloud.

In an instant, Joyce and Felicia were all over each other, smacking, punching, and pulling each other's hair.

Raven remained quiet in the corner as she was used to seeing her mother act out; especially towards her aunt Joyce.

"What the hell?!" Nia said while running full blast down the stairs and charging at her mother, pulling her off her aunt. "You got to go! Get out of my Grandma's house and don't ever come back!"

"Who the hell you think you talking to?! I am your momma!"

"You ain't no momma of mine!" Nia yelled. "Grandma is my momma!"

Trinity screamed louder and Nia turned to her. "Shut up!"

"Get out and take your grown ass child with you!"

Raven looked over at Trinity and then at her grandmother. A feeling of sadness gripped Raven as she watched her grandmother clutch her chest with tears in her eyes and her sister balling her eyes out at the sight of her mother acting up. Thoughts of her younger years flashed into her mind; there were many moments when she was in Trinity's spot, crying loudly for her mother to stop fighting with whoever was in her way. Walking over to her little sister, she reached her hand out and Trinity moved away, rolling her eyes at Raven.

"Raven, don't bother! Let that brat go on with her mother," Nia said as she walked over to the door and opened it, ushering for her mother to walk out.

"Nia! Stop!"

"Well, that's what she is Grandma!"

"Hush up, girl!"

Now it was time for Raven to watch her sister and her grandmother go back forth with each other. Just like their mother, Nia was known to go overboard at times; with anybody at any time, including with their sixty-five-year-old grandmother.

"Don't get slapped girl!"

Raven looked at her grandmother and then back at her sister.

"Let me go!" Nia muttered. "And why are y'all still here?! Get out!" Nia yelled loudly at her mother and her little sister.

Raven frowned at her mother, not realizing that she was still in the house.

"My child had to go to the bathroom! Not that it's any of your business, Nia!"

"Come on baby, let's get out of here and go with our real family."

Raven sadly stared at her mother as she doted on her little sister. *She never treated me like that. What is so wrong with me that I never got her love and attention like that?*

"Come on, your grandmother got some stuff that Santa left for you at her house. Come on baby. Let's get out of this house with these ratchet people."

"Ratchet?! I know you ain't calling us ratchet! You out of all people!"

Raven continued to look on from a distance as her mother walked out of the house, holding her precious little girl and slamming the door behind her. "Humph, there's my good Christmas," she huffed before walking in the kitchen to check up on her aunt Joyce and her grandmother.

CHAPTER 7

"Y ep, I told you I wanted to chill wit' you," Shannon said while closing his front door and sitting down next to Raven on the porch.

Raven smiled at Shannon and then shyly turned away.

"What?" He chuckled. "I know you ain't all shy now."

Raven looked over at Shannon and then back out the window. "Nope, just got a lot on my mind." Thoughts of the fight between her mother and her aunt jumped into her mind, causing her a throbbing headache.

"Was sup?"

"Ugh," she muttered. "Nothing that I feel like talking about. I'm good."

"A'ight."

"Wait! Wait for me!"

Raven smiled at the group of children running down the street, throwing snowballs at each other and riding their bikes all at the same time. The smallest child caught her eye and she kept her eyes on him. The thought of having a baby crept into her mind yet again. *That would be good for me. A baby who would love me and I would love him or her and won't have to worry about nothing. Yep, nothing but taking care of my child.*

"Aye."

Raven turned to Shannon and smiled. "What? I'm right here. Why are you yelling?"

"Why are you staring at that little boy so hard?"

Raven focused her attention on Shannon's face, paying close attention to his eyes. *Hmmm,* she mumbled internally. *His or her daddy's eyes. And for sure would have his jet-black coal hair.*

"What? Was sup with you?"

"Nothing, just thinking." The faint buzzing in her pocket caught her attention. Frowning, she stared at the unfamiliar number on the screen.

"What?"

"I don't know who this is, and I didn't give my number out to anybody but my sis—"

The buzzing of the phone shook Raven's hand, with the same number popping onto the screen.

"Just answer it. It's probably just a wrong number."

"Hello."

"Raven, hey baby."

Sighing, Raven rolled her eyes at the sound of the voice. "Hey Ma."

"Oh, so that's how you act towards me? I was just calling to see if you wanted to come over to my baby's party. But since you are acting all crazy, then never mind." Before Raven could say a word, her mother hung up the phone.

"The hell with you too," she whispered and put her phone on her lap.

"What's wrong?"

"Nothing, just my mother and her crazy ass."

"Oh."

"Yeah, she's just crazy and don't care nothing about nobody except for her precious baby and her baby daddy and his kids. The rest of us can kick rocks as far as she is concerned. You know..." Raven stopped and smiled at Shannon. "Never mind. It's not even worth me talking about it."

"You good. You can talk to me," Shannon replied and touched Raven's leg.

Raven began to feel a bit warm, although the weather was cold, snowy, and gloomy. The warmth took over her entire leg and instantly made its way throughout the rest of her body.

"I know," Raven replied. Not sure of what she should say or do next. The fact that Shannon's hand was touching her made her feel like she was loved and wanted. It was a feeling that she was chasing all her life. Again, the thought of a family; in her mind, a real family entered her thoughts and dominated them.

"So, where is my kiss?"

What?! Raven's mind screamed. *A kiss?* Hearing her sister's voice, she tried hard not to be nervous, even though it was her very first kiss ever. *Girl what is wrong with you?! The boy wants a kiss so go ahead and kiss him already,* Nia's voice screamed loudly in her mind. Quickly before she lost all nerve, she kissed Shannon and stood up. "Okay, I will call you later," she said while walking down the steps and off onto the sidewalk.

Shannon chuckled, stood, and stretched before walking towards his front door. "A'ight. I got to work tonight, so I will call you on my break."

"Okay," Raven said in a rushed voice, not really recognizing herself. *What just happened? I just had my first kiss and now I know. I know what comes next.* Happily, she walked home as she thought of Shannon, the kiss, and a new kind of love.

"Yes! I can't believe he actually kissed me."

"Uh, what did you think would happen?" Nia laughed. "You know y'all would kiss eventually. That's just the beginning."

Raven was so excited that she thought she would burst open into tiny million pieces; an excitement and love that she's never felt before. "I know but—"

"But nothing," Nia cut her sister off. "You now have a boyfriend; a boyfriend with a car and a job. Girl, you doing better than me. That scrub I'm with ain't about nothing. You just make sure you keep him."

Raven shifted her weight on her bed and smiled. "Yep, I will definitely be keeping him."

"Yeah girl, you know..."

Thoughts of a family; a real family entered into Raven's mind, drowning out Nia's entire conversation. Before she knew it, Nia was done talking and yelling her name as if she had lost her mind.

"What?!" Raven shouted back.

"You haven't heard a word I said. So busy thinking about Shannon."

"I did hear you."

"Okay, what did I say about your mother?"

Raven thought of the phone call she'd gotten earlier that day from Felicia and frowned. "Uh, probably the fact that she—"

"Uh huh, you weren't listening to me," Nia laughed. "I know how it is to be in love, girl."

"Whateva, I'm not in love. Just tell me what you were saying."

"Uh huh, I was saying that your mother had the nerve to call Grandma and invite her to some wack ass party she and her brat are having."

"Yeah, she called me too but then she told me not to come and hung up on me."

"Ugh, I can't stand her."

"Yeah," Raven muttered.

"Anyway, I got to go before Grandma starts running her mouth about the dishes. Already started with me earlier today."

Raven laughed. "Well, you better go ahead and get them done then. You know how Grandma can be."

"Yep, I swear they all only took us in so we can work all the time."

"Bye girl," Raven laughed before hanging up her phone.

Laying down on her back, Raven listened to the sound of the washing machine and closed her eyes. A crib and a stroller grabbed her brain's attention. Grabbing her phone, she summoned Google and began her personal research about babies, what to expect when pregnant and pregnancy do's and don'ts.

CHAPTER 8

Welcome back students! I hope you all had a wonderful holiday break. Now it's back to business! The fun stuff!"

Raven sat in her seat and looked at Ms. Carter like she had lost her mind. *Neither Harriet High nor this science class is poppin' like that. I can't wait to get out of here and see my man.* Feeling that warm and tingling feeling all over, she continued to think of Shannon while pretending to be engaged in what Ms. Carter was saying.

"When did this happen?"

Raven looked over at Jasmine and waited for her to answer Jules' question. She really didn't hang out with them, she just walked home with them every day to make her aunt happy. Ensuring that she was safe from the dangers of the streets that a pretty young girl could encounter by walking home all by herself from school. *Yeah, Aunt Joyce don't mind sending me to the store all the time by myself, but she wants to make sure I walk in a group walking home from school.*

Hmmm, she said to herself when her aunt suggested the two *good girls* to walk home with. *Aunt Joyce would lose her mind if she knew what was going on with her pick of girls that she wants me to walk home with every day.*

"Girl, I don't even know. I just know I didn't get my period," Jasmine answered and put her head down, nearly tripping over a patch of black ice.

Raven remained quiet but at the same time, paid very close attention. She already had her plan together but had no idea on what to do to make it her reality. Yes, she knew the basics, but then what? It was just a matter of making sure Shannon was on board and her body was ready to cooperate. The girls stood at the crosswalk and waited for the signal to cross.

"What did your mom say?"

"What did my mom say? Jules, have you bumped your head? What do you mean what did my mom say? I didn't tell her and I'm not going to tell her. I can't walk in the house and say, "Ma, I didn't get my period. She's going to say, now you know I'm not taking care of another one of your kids. You already have one that I have to take care of while you're at school.""

"Yes, you can, and you have to because you're not going to be able to hide this for long."

The flashing hand flashed on the sign, giving the girls the go to walk across the street.

"What about the father? Did you tell him?"

"Nope."

"No...? Jasmine, you have to at least tell him."

"Nope. Not going to do that. He can't be having no babies because he will be going to college next year, so I plan to take care of my baby by myself. I take care of Mia by myself; I don't call her father for nothing. So, I can take care of this one the same way."

Jules looked over at Raven and Raven shrugged her shoulders.

"Do you hear her?"

Again, Raven shrugged her shoulders. "It's her choice," she said softly.

"Thanks girl," Jasmine said and moved closer to Raven. "You understand, don't you?"

Raven nodded her head and kept walking. "I guess if you want to have your baby by yourself, then that's your choice."

"Yo! What is the matter with y'all?! Do y'all know how hard it is to have a baby? My mom had me at fifteen and she's been struggling ever since."

"Well, it's not going to be like that with me," Jasmine said as she readjusted her book bag. "I am going to have my baby and we will be just fine."

"You trippin'. You'll see how hard it is once it's done."

The girls reached another quiet spot in their conversation and Raven's mind when into overdrive with thoughts of her baby. *I wonder what it's like. Is it easy to get pregnant?* She looked over at Jasmine. *I guess so if Jasmine did it and so many other girls at school is already pregnant or already had babies.*

"You said your mom had you when she was young right? You good, so me and my baby will be good."

"I also said she struggled all her life, all our lives. I guess you didn't catch that."

"Wat up Jasmine!"

Jasmine waved her hand and kept walking.

"Wow, so, that's all you and your baby daddy have to say to each other? He says wat up and you wave but yet y'all done went half on a baby."

"Yes, a baby that he doesn't know about. We ain't even together like that anymore anyways."

"I will call you later. Maybe then you will have a little more sense."

"Bye chick," Jasmine replied

"See you tomorrow," Raven added.

"That's why I didn't want to tell her; she always has something to say about everything."

"Yeah," Raven responded.

"Okay, I will see you later."

"Um, what is it like?" Raven blurted out before Jasmine could make it all the way up her steps.

"What's... what... like?"

Raven walked closer. "Being pregnant," she whispered and looked over at Jasmine's front door. "I didn't want to say it all loud," she said and pointed to the ajar door.

Jasmine followed Raven's finger and looked back at her. "Well, it's kind of weird."

Raven laughed nervously and switched her book bag from her right shoulder to her left.

"It's mostly feeling sick all the time and sleepy."

"Oh." *Yeah, I read about that morning sickness.* "Is it bad? I mean, do you ever have to stay in bed or anything like that?"

"Nah, nothing like that. It's ok. I haven't had any cravings or nothing yet."

"Oh." Raven smiled at the message that spread across her phone. "Well, I got to go but I will see you tomorrow." She said quickly to Jasmine but kept her eyes on her phone.

"A'ight."

Hey. She replied to Shannon's text and turned back to Jasmine.

"Hey Jasmine, if you ever need to talk or anything. You can call me."

"Thanks girl," Jasmine said tenderly. "I appreciate that."

Raven texted her number to Jasmine before she restarted her walk through the icy streets to Shannon's house. *Four o'clock,* she read silently from her phone. *Plenty of time before Aunt Joyce gets home.* Thinking of Jasmine and the fact that she hasn't told her baby's father that he was going to be a father bothered Raven. Reaching Shannon's house, Raven's mind thought of how wrong she would be to keep big news like having a baby away from the father. *I don't want to do that to Shannon. Maybe I should tell him today. A baby would be perfect for us and our baby would have the best grandparents...on his side anyway. We've been chillin' for almost two months and already close. All we have to do now is plan it and we...* Raven stopped mid- thought when she spotted Shannon's mom.

"Hey Raven, how are you doing today?"

"Hi Ms. Sharon. I'm okay and you?"

"Doing good love. Shannon went to the store, but he'll be back soon if you want to come in."

"Okay," Raven replied and walked up the steps and into Shannon's house behind his mother. The first thing she looked at each and every time she entered his house was the family pictures on the walls.

"Have a seat baby."

Sitting down on the couch, she imagined a picture of a baby, her baby, on the wall next to his or her father's picture when he was little. Smiling, she stood up and walked over to the wall. *Yep, right there is where we can put our baby's picture. Up there with the rest of the family.*

"Wat up."

"Hey," Raven spoke to Shannon and hugged him.

"How was your day?"

He cares. "It was good. What about yours?"

"It was cool," Shannon answered and sat down on the couch. "I have to get ready to go to the base this weekend."

"What? Why?" Raven sat down beside him.

"It's my turn to go. You know I go one weekend out of the month, and this is my weekend to go."

"Yeah, but you just went—"

"Last month," Shannon laughed. "Was sup?"

Raven thought of the calendar that she had hidden under her mattress; all marked up with the important dates. Dates that she learned from the stories on the internet. "Nothing," she said quickly. "It's just—"

"Wat up, Raven?" Tavon said as he walked into the room.

"Wat up bruh?"

"Was sup, Tavon."

"Hey," Raven spoke.

"What are y'all up to?"

Raven remained quiet as she thought of her calendar and the fact that the one person she needed would be gone out of town.

"Nothing, getting ready to go back and finish packing up."

"Oh, dat's was sup."

"Well, I'm going to go ahead and get home before Aunt Joyce comes home and finds something to complain about."

"Your aunt always be trippin'," Tavon laughed.

"Yep, she does," Raven chuckled.

Raven and Shannon both stood up and walked over to the door.

"A'ight. I'll call you after I get done packing."

"Okay." Raven hugged Shannon and blushed when he kissed her on the forehead. Taking her first step down the stairs, she turned back towards Shannon.

"Hey."

Shannon turned around. "Yeah?"

Going back to the front of the porch, she leaned close to Shannon. "What do you think about kids?"

"Kids? They cool."

"They cool," Raven repeated, suddenly losing her nerve to bring up the subject of them having one of their own.

"Why? That's a crazy question."

"Um, well, I was thinking. I want to..." Raven stopped to give her stomach time to settle; waves of panic and nausea took over. "Never mind," she said instead. "Just call me when you get done with packing your stuff."

"Nah, what is it?"

Raven continued to look at Shannon, but her mouth didn't move.

"Raven, was sup? You good?"

"Um, yeah. I'm good."

Shannon laughed aloud, catching Raven off guard. "Then why are you standing there lookin' all crazy. What is it?"

Just say it, Raven. Her inner voice took full control at this point since her physical mouth was at a standstill. "How do you feel about having kids?" She blurted out, not giving her inner voice and her mouth more time to debate.

Shannon laughed and then shook his head. "Uh um, no kids. At least not for a while. Like a long time from now."

Raven's heart sank. The one thing she wanted to do was have a family of her own with the cutest and most productive, and family-oriented boy she had ever known.

"Why are you asking ... Raven? Please don't tell me that you're—"

"No, no, nothing like that," Raven giggled. Hoping to lighten the mood. "Of course not, I was just wondering." Raven smile turned into an awkward smirk as she watched Shannon's face change from happiness and content to a look resembling frustration.

"A'ight. Don't be messin' with me like that girl. Shoot. I ain't into babies and stuff like that."

"Right. Okay, I better go so you can finish packing."

"Okay baby. I'll call you. Whew! Girl you scared yo' boy for a minute there."

"Dang, okay, I got it. No kids for you," Raven mumbled while turning to walk away, a feeling of defeat taking over.

"Almost home," she began to sing, "No more drama... no, no... not this time..." one of her favorite songs. Singing always, well most of the time, calmed her nerves when she felt embarrassed or ashamed. Reaching the last house before she got to her aunt's, she spotted the infamous pink convertible that everybody in the family always talked about; the Barbie car. *Damn, what is she doing here?* Sighing, she slowed her steps, trying to take as much time as she could before she entered into the house. It wasn't that she didn't want to be see her aunt Charlotte, it was who she undoubtingly brought with her, Carla. If she would just leave her at home... Standing in front of her aunt's car, she looked inside at the pink and black interior. *I'll have a car like this one day. I guess I should get this little visit over with and it's cold out here! I'm not going to keep standing out here in this just because my bitch sister is in the house.* She peered down at the basement steps. *I wonder if Aunt Joyce would give me a key. Then, anytime somebody is over here, I can just go straight to my room.*

"Humph, what am I thinking? She ain't going to give me nothing that would make my life easier." Walking up the steps, she opened the back door and stepped inside, taking her scarf off first, she then reached down to pull her boots off, knowing that her aunt would have her head if she dripped snow in the house. She then took off her coat and hung it on the rack by the door.

"Hey!"

"Hey, Aunt Joyce."

"Ain't you come in and say hi to me too?"

Raven giggled and walked into the living room. "Yes ma'am, I was just taking off my stuff, but I was coming. How you doing, Aunt Charlotte?"

"I'm good dear. How are you? How was school?"

"It was good."

"Okay, that's good."

Raven looked around while her aunt Charlotte continued to make small talk. *What?! She left her home.* Everybody in the family knew how Carla felt about her sisters and how all the sisters felt about her, so it would be strange for Raven to ask about her. Instead, she sat down next to her aunt and enjoyed the moment.

"Yeah, I told Momma that she needs to start taking her medicine on time. She knows she supposed to take it every day at the same time."

"Joyce, you know Momma don't like to listen to nobody. Like she always says, she is older than all of us and she ain't reach that age by being stupid."

"Yep, that's Momma for you. Always carrying on about how she's the oldest so that makes her right about everything."

Raven yawned and stood up. "I got homework so I'm going to go ahead and get started."

"Okay baby, you need to come and visit me and your Uncle Charles sometime. We would love to have you over. Maybe even spend the night with us."

Is the bitch going to be there? Cause if she's going to be there, then we can kill all that spending the night. "Yeah, okay," she said and hugged her aunt.

"I'm frying some fish for dinner. It'll be ready soon." Joyce said as she rubbed her left knee.

"Okay," Raven turned and smiled before walking towards the basement. Going down the stairs, she stopped on the third step and listened. She heard some paper or something that sounded like paper rattling. "Aye!" She said and waited for an answer. She looked back the top of the stairs and then back down the stairs. A rush of adrenaline took over and she walked the rest of the way down the stairs. "Ugh! Shit!" Holding her chest, she waited for her breathing to return to normal before she spoke. "You scared me! What the hell are you doing down here?!" Raven looked over to her dresser and her bed and then back at Carla. "I'm only going to ask you this one more time. What are you doing down here?! With all my stuff?!"

Carla rolled her eyes and didn't say a word. She whipped past Raven, walked up the stairs like she was all alone, and didn't have a care in the world.

"Did that heffa' just ignore me?" She turned to see her sister reach the last step and then stepped foot into the kitchen before she slammed the door behind her.

"Don't come back down here, Trick!" *What the hell was she doing down here anyways?* Raven thought. Huffing, she walked over to her bed, threw her book bag down on the floor and flopped down. Nothing seemed out of place, so she calmed down. *She better not had been messing with any of my stuff. I can't stand her.* Buzzing from the dryer rang out, startling

Raven all over again. She jumped and put her hands over her head.

"Damn! I swear that lady keeps that thing on just to annoy me!" Rushing over to the dryer, she hastily opened the door and pulled out the contents inside. *Towels*. "Well, at least it ain't a bunch of old grandma panties." Feeling a bit better, she took a long deep breath, quickly folded up the towels, and placed them on top of the dryer. She then walked back to her bed, sat down, and thought of Shannon.

His words, *no babies*, echoed through her mind. *Why not Shannon? We would have a pretty baby... and a family*. Laying back, she looked towards the stairs and thought of the life that her uncle Charles had with his lucky wife, Charlotte. *We can be just like them, if not better. Why not Shannon?* She asked herself again before picking up her calendar and a pen. She opened it to the place where she had her plan mapped out. All her "O" days she had circled in the book, she marked out with her black pen and threw it on the floor. "So much for that. All that researching I did to even learn how to calculate all that." Sighing, she closed her eyes and flushed out all the thoughts; thoughts of Carla, her life as the one who got stuck with aunt Joyce and her basement, and Shannon's painful rejection. She closed her eyes tighter and waited to fall asleep. The only way she knew how to escape.

CHAPTER 9

I had it first! "

"Give it back!"

"Both of y'all better go somewhere and sit down! Before I knock both of y'all out!"

Raven shook her head at Nia while she was yelling at their two little cousins from North Carolina.

"They are getting on my nerves. I don't even know why Aunt Bunny had to bring them."

"Um, because they are her grandkids," Raven chuckled.

"Right, her grandchildren. Not her kids. She should've left them at home with their mom or somebody."

"Oh," Raven mumbled. *Maybe it was something that I ate.* Holding her stomach, she felt as if she was going to be sick. Right in front of her sister and her cousins; no time to make it to her grandmother's bathroom. Jumping up off the chair, she ran towards the bathroom and then stopped.

"Girl, what in the world is wrong with you?"

Raven looked at Nia and then removed her hand from her mouth. "False alarm," she quipped. Walking back over to the couch, she sat down and put her head in her hands. The room felt as if it was spinning and she was going to fall out of the chair and onto the floor at any given minute. "I'm not feeling so good; probably something I ate."

"Something you ate. Why don't I believe... oh, Raven?"

Raven slowly looked up at her sister. "What?"

"Did you and Shannon—?"

"Shhh, what does that have to do with anything?"

"Oh my gosh! Why didn't you tell me about that?! I should—"

"Can you please shut up?! Why are you so loud with it?"

"I can't believe you! Why didn't you—"

"Let's go to your room...before your big mouth calls somebody in here!"

Raven shook her head while watching her sister run up the stairs. Walking behind her, she turned to see her two little cousins pushing each other and trying to snatch toys out of each other's hands. *I can have just one, so I don't deal with that.* Walking up the stairs and towards her sister's bedroom was like walking with weights strapped to both ankles; she dreaded going in there and undoubtedly being drilled and interrogated.

"Raven!"

"I'm coming, Trick!" Raven yelled. "What?!" She said while closing the door.

"What do you mean, "What?!" Did y'all do it or not!"

Raven flopped down on the floor and looked out the window. More snow began to fall, and the sky was darker than it had been a few hours earlier, indicating yet another snowstorm. "Yeah," she said shyly.

Raven giggled at the sight of Nia's face; her mouth was as wide open as the ocean and she looked like her eyes were going to pop out of her head.

"When?!"

"Why is that important?"

Holding her head, Raven frowned as she began to feel dizzy, hot, and nauseous, a feeling that she had for a couple of weeks but yet, felt as if she was just experiencing it all beginning yesterday. *I hate this part of it*, she thought to herself as her sister continued to ask a million and one questions that she was now tuning out.

"Uh oh, you okay?"

Raven looked at Nia and shook her head no. "I haven't been feeling good; I think I might be getting the flu or something."

"Or you could be pregnant. Damn Raven, did y'all use any—?"

Raven put her hand up to stop her sister. *Protection would've jacked my plan all the way up so no.* Instead of saying what was really on her mind, she walked over to the window and opened it, hoping that the fresh, cold air would stop some of her symptoms.

"Girl, you crazy?! It's cold as hell outside! Shut that window!"

"Uh, if it was like hell, wouldn't it be the other way around?" Raven laughed.

"Shut up, you know what I mean and if you don't start giving me some details, I'm going to send you there and you will be more than just warm."

Raven giggled, shook her head, and closed the window.

"So, when... what... how...?"

Raven sat down on the floor. "I like him, and he likes me, so we went there. It happened a few weeks ago, and I'm not getting into the how," Raven smacked her lips at her sister's look of anxiousness. "You ain't innocent so figure that part out."

"I cannot believe my little sister had her first...wait, it was your first time, right?"

Raven put her head down and pulled one of the pillows her sister kept lined on her bed and cradled it.

"Raven?!"

"What?!"

"Tell me that it was your first—"

"My second!" She yelled before looking towards her sister's door. *So many people are over here; anybody could be standing at the door listening and being all nosey.*

"Second? What do you mean second? When was the first time and with who?"

Throwing the pillow back on the bed, and fighting another wave of nausea, she put her head down. "With him and a few weeks before the second time."

"Okay, you scared me for a minute there. I thought you was with somebody else before him. That's good that it was only with him. What about protection? Did y'all use protection?"

"No."

"No! Oh, Raven. Why not?"

"Nia! Raven! Y'all come on and eat!"

The sight, smell, and even talks of food made Raven feel like she was going to be swallowed completely by her stomach. "I can't eat anything," she said aloud, forgetting that her sister was there in her face, watching her every move.

"Let's go to the store and get a test."

"What?"

"A test. Let's go."

Raven looked outside. "We can't go now; it's getting ready to snow again."

"So! What does the weather have to do with you finding out if you're pregnant?"

"Hey! Y'all come on!"

"Ugh, damn it, Grandma. We are coming!" Nia yelled.

"You better had kept that first part low so Grandma couldn't hear you," Raven giggled. "You going to mess around and get slapped."

"Shut up and come on."

Raven stood up slowly and followed her sister out of her room and down the stairs. She frowned at her two little cousins as they continued to fight, this time, over which channel to watch.

"Girl, I hope you don't have to deal with demon seeds like them," Nia quipped while putting on her coat.

Raven looked around, hoping that nobody of age was around to hear her sister's comment.

"Just turn it back!"

"No! I want to watch this!"

Raven shook her head at her cousins and placed her hands on her head, hoping to remove the dizziness that was beginning spread across face.

"Grandma! I got to go to the store..."

"Raven, get your coat on. Just standing there looking all crazy."

"I'll be back!"

Pulling her coat off the couch, Raven followed Nia's orders and quickly slid it on.

"Where you going?!"

"I have to run to the store. Raven is going with me."

"What y'all need at the store so bad that y'all have to go out in the snow?" Joyce peered into the living room and frowned.

"I have to get some—"

"Pads, Aunt Joyce," Nia jumped in and looked at Raven.

Raven smiled at her aunt, hoping to take that look of *"they think I'm stupid"* look off her face.

"How y'all getting there?"

"Uh, I guess my...car."

Raven giggled at her sister's sarcasm but quickly turned straight-faced when her aunt Joyce looked at her as if she was getting ready to smack all sense out of her.

"Don't get cute, Nia."

"I wasn't trying to be," Nia said as she pushed her long weave out of her face.

"Come on girl; let's go before your aunt has a fit."

"Momma, you better get that chile before I snatch all the sense out of her!"

Raven grabbed her scarf off the chair and loosely threw it across her neck as she walked quickly to the door and opened it. "Come on Nia, let's ride."

"Oh," she mumbled as she began with the feeling of dizziness followed by a wave of nausea, much smaller than all the previous times. Walking onto the porch, thoughts of Shannon entered into her mind. *Maybe I should call him. I probably shouldn't*

"Come on!"

Sighing and rolling her eyes, she jogged out in her grandmother's yard and joined Nia in the car.

"Damn, it's cold out here!"

"Yeah," Raven agreed. Beginning to get nervous, she looked over at her sister. "Maybe we shouldn't go and buy that. I don't feel all that bad and it's not time for my period. Maybe we should—"

"Shut it. We are going and you are going to take it."

Becoming quiet, Raven thought of the result to her actions. Shannon doesn't want a baby. *What if I have to do all this by myself... maybe it's negative... but then...* her thoughts stopped when the car came to a halt. Although the ride was only around twenty minutes or so, the entire drive felt like it was only a few seconds as Raven was in her thoughts and her feelings throughout the entire ride. Hesitating, she opened her door, got out, and followed behind Nia into the drug store.

"Dang, how do you know exactly where it is?" Raven frowned.

"That's none of your business; just find one and come on."

All brands, colors, types, and prices shot out at Raven like the brightest star in the sky and she was somebody looking to identify which one of the great stars it was. "So many, I don't know which one to pick." Looking over at her sister, she sighed.

"Raven, just pick—"

"I don't know which one!"

"Ugh," Nia yelled as she grabbed one of the pink boxes and walked towards the cashier, leaving Raven behind.

"Ohh-kayyy."

Walking to catch up with her sister, she waited while Nia paid for the test; feeling a sense of embarrassment while she waited.

"See, that's all to it. You standing there like you have no sense at all. Come on; let's go before Grandma starts blowin' my phone up."

Raven thought of Shannon as she walked out of the drug store.

CHAPTER 10

Surprise! We are going to have a baby... Yo, you know I got your seed now! "Nah, that's wack as hell." Raven stood in the mirror and frowned. *Why did I do this?* She held her stomach as waves of emotion came over her. Turning away from the mirror, she walked out of the bathroom and looked into her aunt's bedroom. The TV played with no sound as her aunt slept. *I wonder what she would have to say when she finds out about this.*

Walking down the stairs, she sighed as she made her way through the living room, and then kitchen before going down into the basement. Flopping down on the bed, she grabbed a pillow and slid it slowly under her shirt while looking at her reflection in the basement's window. "So... this is what I will look like in a few months. Cute," she hoarsely said before removing the pillow and throwing it on the bed. Sighing again, this time louder than before she spotted her phone and the blinking light that was coming from it. *A message? When did it go off?* Laying across her bed, she grabbed her phone and was delighted to see a new message from Shannon.

Aye.

"Aye, that's it," she giggled. "Maybe I should make him wait a minute before I text him back." A wave of nausea followed by a faint feeling of lightheadedness came over her body and she gasped. This time, the nausea was stronger and deeper than all the other times. Holding her mouth, she ran towards the steps and sat down on the first one. "False alarm," she mumbled as the wave disappeared.

Hey. She typed in before another wave of nausea began.

Shannon's smile entered into her mind followed by a frown and the look of pure anger when she had to tell him that she was having a baby; his baby. *What is he going to say? He already said he didn't want...*

Wya...

Why Raven? She continued with her mental rant while slowly rubbing her belly. Getting up off the step, she walked back over to her bed and flopped down. *Why did I do this?*

Home.

I wonder what his mom is going to say. What my mom is going to... well, she don't really matter. She is so busy having a life with her man and his family; she could care less about being a grandmother.

Come out... on my way.

"Ugh, no, not right now. I still have to figure out... this is so messed up," She admitted to herself. *Well, you did it. You should've used some type of protection*, she heard Nia's voice scolding her. *I did it on purpose; been planning it for months*, she was thinking while her sister was yelling at her at the exact moment the little stick turned from clear to the infamous pink lines in the middle. "Maybe Nia is right; it's a false positive. I wish I could go back and do it all over again."

Yes, she wanted a baby at one point, but now that she was faced with the reality of actually having one, her mind and her judgment said otherwise. She now felt an incredible sense of dread and fear;

127

especially since she was faced with the possibility of raising a baby on her own as Shannon already told her that he wasn't ready for kids.

Wya

Sighing, she pulled her coat down off the washing machine and slowly walked up the stairs and out the back door. A feeling of dread took over her instead of the feelings she normally felt when she saw Shannon, or anything affiliated with him. She walked slowly as her boots crunched the old snow that had fallen earlier in the day.

"Was sup?"

"Hey," she said in a whispered tone as she got into the passenger seat.

"What's wrong?"

"Huh? Oh, nothing," she lied. "Just sleepy."

"A'ight. I just wanted to see you before I got to work."

"K, call me on your break."

"A'ight."

Giving him a quick peck, Raven unusually rushed out of the car as fast as she could, not really wanting to be around him due to the incredible guilt she was feeling. Turning to give a wave, she walked back to the house with tears in her eyes.

"So, did you tell him?"

"Um... tell...him...what?"

"Um," Nia mocked. "About the baby?"

Raven leaned against her grandmother's kitchen counter and put her head down.

"You didn't."

"No, I did– shut up before somebody hears you." Looking into the living room, she frowned at her two little cousins who were still visiting from North Carolina. "When are they leaving?"

"Girl, forget them and let's talk about why you didn't tell that boy that you—"

"Cause, it wasn't time and I'm not even sure. The magazine said that I should go to the doctor before I-"

"Magazine? Since when do you read magazines? And what magazine is going to tell you like your big sister?"

"People who've been there and done that. You don't have any experience besides scares and you just waited for your period—"

"A'ight, point made. But, you still need to make sure you tell him. You sure can't go to the doctor and-"

"Nia, I'm thirsty."

"Me too."

"Why y'all in here?! Go back in the living room until your grandma comes back."

"But I'm thir—"

"Yeah, I heard you the first time," Nia spat. "Now go back into the—"

"Really Nia?"

Raven rolled her eyes and grabbed two plastic cups from the table.

"Here y'all," she said as she opened the refrigerator and poured cherry soda into their cups. She watched as the boys gulped the drinks down and ran back into the living room

"Huh, they didn't even say thank you."

"Girl that's why I don't deal with them. I don't even know why they left them here with us in the first place. Knowing how they are, there grandmother should've taken them with her."

"You know how long Grandma can be when she's looking for something for church. It can take her hours and she walks way too slow."

"Uh uh, not now girl," Nia chuckled. She gets in them scooters now, so she be ridin'."

Raven laughed, "Those things are slow as hell too so—"

"Y'all come and help us with the bags!"

"Dang, must your aunt be so loud."

"Our aunt."

"Whateva."

Pulling her shirt down to cover her hips, Raven followed Nia out the back door and to her aunt's car. Picking up a bag, the old pesky feeling was back, rolling around in her stomach but she swallowed hard a few times and walked to the door anyway, trying her hardest to ignore it.

"Where them boys at?"

"Boys, y'all come on out here and help get some of these bags!" Joyce yelled at the top of her lungs.

Raven laughed at Nia as she frowned and shook her head. "She really doesn't have to be that loud. I mean, we are all a few steps away."

"Girl ignore it and let's finish getting these bags so I can go home and go to bed," Raven chuckled.

"You got it Momma? You want one of these girls to help you get up the stairs?"

Oh no! I can't hold bags, my stomach, and Grandma all at the same time.

"Nah, I can make it up there."

Good, I don't think I can keep standing, let alone help an old lady up the stairs. We will mess around and both of us fall.

"Yeah, I got it."

"Okay, Momma."

"Well, y'all bring the rest of the bags in. I got to get Momma's meds ready before I go," Joyce said.

"Boys! Where are y'all at?! Y'all quit running around this house and help with the bags!"

Raven walked behind Nia as they brought the last of the grocery's and other bags into the house.

"We got them already now, Aunt Joyce," Nia said and rolled her eyes at her aunt. "No need to keep calling them."

"Where in the world did they go?!" Joyce muttered as she sat one of the bags on the kitchen table.

"I know they better not be in my room!" Nia yelled. "Aye!"

Raven shook her head, walked into the living room, sat down on the couch, and flashed a quick smile at her grandmother.

"Chile, what's wrong with you? I've been noticing that you don't look right."

"Huh?" Raven looked over at her sister and her sister turned the other way.

"Nothing Grandma, I'm all good."

"Okay, just making sure. You talk to your momma?"

Thoughts of her mother and the loveless relationship she'd had with her because she didn't belong to her boyfriend danced around in her head, causing her to feel dizzy. "No ma'am."

"Why would she talk to her?" Nia asked harshly before flopping down on the couch beside Raven. "All she cares about is that little brat she has with her drug dealer boyfriend."

"That's still yo' momma."

"Well, she ain't no momma of mine."

"Y'all need to call her more and spend time with her. She is still y'all momma."

My own baby; my own family. Raven tuned her grandmother out as she thought of the baby, well, potential baby that was growing inside of her. Reading the articles in *Intuitions Magazine* kept Raven in her thoughts. Although the magazine was local and really didn't have a lot of clout yet, it had some interesting stories with educated, well trained, people writing them. *You must go to an OBGYN to make sure. There are known false positives so be sure to get to your doctor's office. Wait, I don't even have a doctor. How would I do it? Where would I go?*

"What is this?!"

Raven flipped back into her reality, remembering that she was sitting in the living room with her family and her grandmother talking about why she and all four of her sisters should be close with their mother.

"Where did you get this from?!"

"I told y'all to stay out of my room!" Nia snapped as she walked over swiftly and pushed one of her cousins.

Raven began to feel faint, nauseated, with a headache, and numbness in her legs all at the same time at the sight of what her aunt Joyce was holding in her hands... **THE POSITIVE PREGNANCY TEST!**

CHAPTER 11

I guess if you would've been around more, then this kind of thing wouldn't have happened."

Raven sat still in one of the hard, blue chairs that lined the walls at the Cove Village Health Department; thirty minutes away from the health department in her neighborhood. *I'm not going to have you embarrass me and take you to a place where I used to work. Oh no, no ma'am!* She thought of the harsh tone that her aunt had used with her a few days after she was done giving her the silent treatment. *All because one of those demons went all up in Nia's room and got the stick out of the trash. Who even gets a pee stick out of the trash and carry it around anyway?* Raven's mind was swirling around in circles while her aunt and her mother continued their spat, in front of everybody waiting in the waiting room.

"Well, Joyce, she is living with you so, who fault is it?"

"Don't make me smack you! That is your child and I ain't got to—"

"Mayz!"

Raven stood up at the sound of her name, looking behind her before she went forward. Her aunt and her mother both sat in their seats, not bothering to walk with her. *The least they could do is stop arguing for five minutes while I go back here and get the test results.*

"Hi, how are you doing?"

"Good," Raven spoke softly to the nurse as the door closed behind her.

"That's good. We are going to go in room three and Doctor Bass will be in shortly to talk to you. Here's your packet with everything you need to know about your baby. The stages of each—"

"Wait, um, so the test was positive?"

"Yep," the nurse said nonchalantly.

A wave of panic, surprise, nervousness, and anxiousness filled her body all at once. She sat down in the chair across from the exam table and held her head in her hands.

"Hey, you okay?"

For some reason, the feeling of embarrassment had now taken over her, making it hard to look up at the nurse. "Yeah," she sniffled. Tears began to trickle down her face as the embarrassment began to get stronger, surpassing all the other feelings. Thoughts of Shannon and the fact that he'd told her that he didn't want any kids popped strongly into her mind.

"You know, you are going to be alright."

"I guess," Raven replied through her sobs.

"Yes, you are," the nurse said and sat down next to Raven, slowly rubbing her back. While the nurse rubbed, the tears fell, and Raven cried harder than she had ever cried before.

"You know, I was a teenage mother, and everything turned out okay for me, so it will turn out okay for you. Is the father around?"

Shannon's smile and the mop of black curly hair flashed first followed by the sound of him saying that he didn't want to be a father maneuvered back into her mind. "Yes... no... I don't know."

"Well, hopefully he will be around to support you during your pregnancy."

"Pregnancy," Raven recited. "What did I do?" She mumbled as the door opened and the doctor walked in.

"Raven, I'm Doctor Bass. Before I get started, we would need your parent or guardian in here. Are they in the waiting room?"

"I'll go and get them," the nurse said as she stood up and started towards the door.

"No!"

Both Dr. Bass and the nurse looked at Raven with startled looks.

"What's the matter?"

Raven hesitated before she admitted the truth. "I-I don't want them in here. They will only cause more problems and stress." *Intuitions Magazine said that pregnant women have to stay away from stressful stuff, so I can't let them come up in here.*

"Are there any problems with abuse or anything like that?" Dr. Bass asked while the nurse pulled out a piece of paper and some pamphlets from the desk.

"No, nothing like that. It's just... well... they are only going to come in and start arguing with each other. They are always fussing about something."

"Hmmm. I understand that they make you upset, but we need a guardian in the room. Who's out there waiting on you?"

Ugh, my crazy Aunt Joyce and my don't care about nothing or nobody unless it's my man and my baby with him momma. "My mother and my aunt," She shyly said instead of blurting out the first thing that came to mind.

"Okay, so, out of the two, which is the calmer one?"

"Humph, neither of them."

The room grew silent for a few seconds.

"Um, I can call my sister."

"Okay, is she eighteen or older?"

Raven put her head down. "Not yet, but she will be in a few months."

"Okay."

"Pam, go out and see if you can get one of her relatives to come back with her."

"Okay, be right back."

"No, I don't—"

"I know, but we have to have a parent or guardian in here with you due to your age. How are you feeling physically?"

Raven sighed loudly and cradled her head in her hands. "Fine, I guess."

"Well, that's good."

Raven watched as the doctor scribbled on a notepad.

"Girl, you really have made a mistake," Joyce sneered as she walked in behind the nurse. "You just couldn't be better than your mother."

Why did they choose her to come in here? I wish my mother would've shown some love for me just this one time and came in here. Why did the nurse get her?

"Your momma left."

Well, there it is. The heffa' left. She didn't have the decency to stay for the appointment. I bet she had something to do with that crazy dude she's with and her daughter; her real daughter.

"I'm Doctor Bass. Thank you for agreeing to come—"

"I didn't agree to nothing! Her sorry momma left so I was the only one out there."

The doctor shook his head and looked at Raven, no longer bothering to have a conversation with Joyce.

"Okay, so you are right at twelve weeks and two days. You will need to start prenatal vitamins. I will give you a prescription before you go."

"She doesn't have any insurance. So, I don't know how she's going to pay for it. I don't have any extra money to pay for some medicine that she wouldn't need if she would've just kept her legs closed."

Dr. Bass and the nurse both looked at Joyce and quickly turned their attention back to Raven.

"We have some here that we can give you. Don't worry about going to the pharmacy."

Raven smiled at the nurse. "Thanks."

"You're very welcome."

Wya...

Raven waited for the nurse to walk out of the room and the doctor to start writing on his notepad again before she responded to Shannon's text. *What do I say? I can't tell him that I'm at the doctor's office. Well, he doesn't have to know why I'm here.*

At the doctor...

"Okay so once Pam gets back with your vitamins, she will set you up for an ultrasound and a prenatal appointment."

"Now, you mentioned you don't have insurance." Dr. Bass looked over at Joyce.

"She doesn't have any insurance, but I do."

"I see," Dr. Bass responded and scribbled something on the notepad.

"Okay, Raven. Then you can come here for your care. We'll see you in a few weeks."

Raven rolled her eyes at her aunt while she hastily walked out of the room. "I'll be in the car," she said before slamming the door behind her. The nurse walked in with a frown on her face.

"Here you go, honey. Be sure to take one every day and call us if you need us. I figured you might need to start your care here instead of a private practice, so Lisa has your appointment information at the front desk. Stop by to see her before you leave."

Why...

Raven looked down at her phone and looked back at the nurse. "Thank you."

"You're welcome. We'll see you in a few weeks."

"Okay," Raven said before walking out into the lobby. Stopping at the front desk, she gave a half smile to the receptionist and waited quietly while she typed into the computer.

"We'll see you in four weeks for your visit," the receptionist said while handing a card to Raven. "Have a nice day."

"Thanks." Walking towards the door, Raven stopped and glanced at her phone. The message from Shannon was still on the screen. Stuffing her phone in her pocket, she walked out the door, preparing herself for another round of silent treatment from her aunt.

CHAPTER 12

"What did you just say?"

Raven kept her eyes focused on the wall as Shannon's mother asked her questions. The same lady she'd come to know as sweet, patient, and kind was now replaced with a woman filled with disgust, frustration, and anger. Shannon looked like he'd just seen Tupac's ghost standing on the other side of the room, and Joyce watched in disappointment.

"Did you say pregnant?"

"Yup, that's what she said. Now, what are y'all going to do about it? I don't have money for a baby and all that."

"Joyce let's hold on with all that for a minute. This child just told us that she was pregnant, right?"

"Yeah, that's right."

Raven stood on the other side of the living room, as far away from Shannon as she could be. The look on his face scared her and she didn't want to be close to him when he finally says something.

"Well, we know who the mother is, but who's the father?"

Ravens knees buckled at the sound of that question. "Huh?" She asked in a hoarse whisper.

"Are you sure my son is the father?"

Raven looked at Shannon and Shannon turned his head. She gasped and put her head down.

"That's a good question," Joyce said, adding extra fuel to the growing fire that was beginning to rage within Raven's stomach.

Did she really just ask that question? And is Shannon really sitting there like he has no idea who my baby daddy is?

"I'm only coming over here for my sister and then after I make sure she's alright, I'm leaving."

"Nia!" Raven called out at the sound of her sister's voice, the only comfort she had at the present time. Jogging over to the door, she pulled it open to allow her sister and her aunt Charlotte to come in.

"You alright?"

"No," Raven answered while trying to keep the tears that were beginning to fall in instead of coming out.

"Of course, she ain't alright. She's a sixteen-year-old mother!" Her aunt Charlotte yelled.

"And Joyce, how you let this happen to the child? She lives with you so—"

"Yeah, but she has a mother. I just let her stay here so she wouldn't be out in the streets. Nobody said nothing about watching her."

"Really?!" Nia yelled and rolled her eyes.

Raven sat down on the couch next to her sister and sighed.

"You wrong for this, Joyce... Just wrong. You know Felicia don't care nothing about what her children are doing. You know that. The girl needs somebody in her corner besides Nia."

Raven couldn't believe that her aunt Charlotte was defending her the way that she was. She looked over at Shannon and Shannon kept his head down. The feeling of defeat replaced the scared feeling she was feeling earlier, when she first broke the news.

"Carla is staying with me and I know that she needs more than just a roof over her head; she needs guidance too, Joyce. All of Felicia's girls do so they won't turn out like her."

"That is not my job. Now, I agreed to take her in and that's it."

"Excuse me!"

The entire room looked at Shannon's mother.

"Can we get back to why me and my son are here? Y'all can talk about family stuff later."

"Oh no she didn't," Nia huffed. "My sister got a part of your family in her stomach."

"Uh-uh, nope! We don't know that yet. We need a DNA test before I start calling that baby my grandchild."

Is she serious right now? The same women who told me that I can talk to her about anything, anytime is now treating me like I'm so hoe off the street. Really?
"Okay, I have nothing to hide. Your son knows it's his baby and you know it too, so whateva."

"Yeah," Nia agreed and put her arm around her sister.

"I guess we'll see." Shannon's mom said and rolled her eyes.

"Yep, we sure will." Nia stared Shannon's mom down, daring her to say anything else.

Raven watched in silence as Shannon and his mother walked out of the house, not bothering to say a word to anybody.

"What is wrong with them?" Nia asked harshly as she shifted her weight on the couch.

Raven put her head down. Feeling the feeling of shame and embarrassment. "I don't know what's wrong with them."

"I do!"

Raven cringed at the sound of her aunt Joyce's voice. "The boy ain't trying to be nobody daddy. He got stuff going on in his life and he ain't going to let you or nobody else mess it up."

"Oh, so this is all Raven's fault?" Charlotte stepped in. "Shannon didn't do anything at all wrong huh?"

"I'm not saying that. I'm just saying that a young boy like him don't have time for babies. Raven should've made sure he used protection then she wouldn't be—"

"Stop Joyce! It takes two and Raven didn't do it by herself. Why didn't he take the initiative to protect himself? Why are you putting it all on Raven?" Charlotte argued back.

Raven put her hand on her stomach, trying to calm the rumble of nausea that was forming before it got out of hand. She tried to tune her family out, but them talking about her, as if she wasn't even in the room, began to take its toll on her.

"I'ma send her to stay with her momma. Felicia need to be the one dealing with this."

"Uh—uh, she ain't going over there. If you don't want her here, she can come to grandma house with me. You know what..." Nia stood up and rolled her eyes at Joyce. "Raven go in that raggedy ass basement and get your stuff. I'm taking you with me to grandma's house."

"The basement? Raven, why is your stuff in the basement?"

"You didn't know, Aunt Charlotte? Your sister-in-law makes Raven sleep down in the basement. Even though she has an extra room upstairs."

"Why Joyce?"

"Because it's my house and I don't want nobody in my room upstairs."

Raven stood up and smirked when she saw the look on her aunt Charlotte's face. The truth was out about how her aunt Joyce really felt about taking her in. She was hoping for a check from the state and when she didn't get it, she completely flipped on Raven; treating her like a stranger that she'd just met instead of her baby sister's daughter.

"Joyce, you should be ashamed of yourself! Does Felicia know that her daughter is—?"

"Pregnant? Nah, her sorry behind left before the doctors came out to get us. She doesn't know about nothing."

"Okay, does she know that you have her daughter sleeping in your basement?"

"What is it about the basement that got y'all so mad?! At least she is sleeping somewhere! Her momma didn't want her at her house, so I did her a favor."

Raven locked eyes with her aunt Charlotte.

"Raven, go and get your stuff, baby. Nia is right; you can go over to your grandmother's house and stay. I guess I have to go down to the school and get you transferred."

School... the least of my problems. "It's okay, I can catch the bus to school from Grandma's house. The number ten stops right down the street from Grandma's house and it goes all the way to my school's area so I can just do that," Raven answered before she retreated to her bedroom, well, the basement to get all of her belongings, intending to never come back to her aunt's house again.

CHAPTER 13

Raven looked around at the people on the crowded bus and sighed; standing and holding on to the rail for dear life as the bus rounded a corner, causing everybody to tip over slightly. Who knew the bus would be this crowded at six o'clock in the morning? Looking out the window, she focused on the dirty piles of old snow that sat on the edges of each street. The sun was slowly rising, and Baltimore was waking up, some people driving around in their cars while others commuted on foot.

You would think one of these men would get up and let me sit down. They can clearly see my stomach pushed out a little bit.

"Aye, you can sit down," a man wearing a suit said as he got up and moved over to the side, grabbing onto one of the bars that lined the top of the bus.

"Thanks." *It's about time somebody offer the pregnant girl a seat.* The window was no longer in view, so she rode the rest of the way to school, in silence, thinking of baby names.

"Third lunch, why did they give me third lunch? Nobody to talk to in here." Raven put her books on the table and pushed her lunch tray away from her. The aroma from the Salisbury steak, well, Harriet High's rendition of the meat, sent waves of nausea throughout her stomach; a feeling that she could never get used to. Looking at her phone, she sighed. *Shannon is still acting funny. I would've thought he would've texted me by now. It's been a whole month since I've talked to him and since him and his mom walked out of Aunt Joyce's house like my baby didn't matter at all.* "Seventeen weeks this week and your father doesn't even know how much you've grown," she whispered and lightly patted her stomach. *I can't believe that bastard done me dirty like this.*

"Hey chick. Since when do you have third lunch?"

"Since the office mixed my schedule up and threw me in here. Whatchu been up to?"

"Nothing, Mia is sick, so I've been dealing with that. Her asthma has been acting up," Jasmine said while throwing her books on the table and sitting across from Raven.

"Aww, I hope she feels better soon."

"Yeah. So, what's been going on with you?"

Raven hesitated; *I don't talk to her like that. Should I tell her? Well, she does have a child already, maybe she can help me figure some stuff out.* "Getting ready to start getting stuff for... my baby."

"Say word?"

"Yeah, I will be seventeen weeks this week."

"Whaattt?! You not even—"

"Showing that much...yeah, I know." *I can sure tell a big difference in my body though. Even though nobody else notices.*

"You should start showing more in the next couple of weeks. Damn. I didn't know you got down like that," Jasmine laughed.

I don't! "Me and my boyfriend...my baby daddy, didn't use protection so I got pregnant."

"I know all about that. That's how Mia got here and ever since I had that scare a few months ago, I went and got on the pill."

"Yeah, I remember that. I remember you saying that you didn't get your period."

"Girl, it came on like a couple of days later. I was happy as shit."

Raven laughed. "That's a saying for you."

Jasmine chuckled, "Yeah girl. I ain't trying to have no more babies. And then got to hear my mom's mouth about it."

"Yo, sit down before I knock yo' ass out!"

Both girls turned towards the commotion to see two boys squaring off.

"Coop need to sit his ass down somewhere. He always up in somebody face."

Raven laughed and shook her head.

"Hey, hey! Y'all both cut that out before I send both of y'all down to the office!"

"Look, watch he sit down now that Mr. Mack caught him. Acting like he 'bout that life."

"I know right?"

"So, do you know what you're having yet?"

"No, the doctor said that we will be able to tell at my next ultrasound appointment. Can't wait for that!"

"Well, if you're having a girl, I can give you Mia's old stuff. It's just sitting in my room in my closet."

"Okay, thanks."

"Yep. She's two; she won't be needing them anymore. Just sitting there, crowding up my closet."

"I appreciate that."

"So, your baby daddy. Does he go here?"

The same Shannon that used to make her smile and get all crazy, now caused her a headache anytime she thought of him or somebody said something about him.

"Nah, he graduated already. He works at the post office and in the Army Reserves."

"Whaatt?! Dat's was sup. You got a man with a—"

"No, just my baby daddy."

"Oh, one of them."

"Him and his mom been acting stupid towards me ever since they found out about my baby."

Raven began to relax and was glad that she decided to tell Jasmine about her pregnancy. It felt good to have somebody to talk to that could relate to her and all the things that she was experiencing. Even down to the absent father.

"Girl don't worry about him or his momma. You will take care of your baby all by yourself and your aunt will help—"

"Nope, she started acting a fool too, so now I live with my grandmother and my sister."

"Damn. It's crazy how people start trippin' when a baby is involved."

"Yep," Raven said softly as she looked at her tray and pushed it further away from her. "The only ones who really ain't trippin' is my grandmother, my sister, and my Aunt Charlotte."

"Oh okay, so at least you got some support."

"I'm glad about that. Not everybody is pissed off at me and then I will have somebody to watch the baby while I come here."

"You do know that you can bring the baby here with you?"

"Yeah but I don't have a job yet so I can't pay—"

"Girl... pay...? You don't have to pay nothing for that."

"You don't?"

"No, I wish they would charge somebody in there."

Space in Raven's mind and her life just got so much easier with the fact that she could bring her baby to school with her. *Yeah, Nia and Aunt Charlotte said they would keep the baby for me, but Nia is looking for a job and Aunt Charlotte smokes.*

"What do I do to get set up?"

"Just fill out the form. They keep them in the office. Just ask for Ms. Deans and she will give you one. I can go with you if you want me to."

"Okay, thanks."

"You're welcome."

Any feeling of uncertainty was now replaced by a comfort that she hadn't felt in a long time; a girl her age and a new friend that she could actually trust.

CHAPTER 14

I remember when I was having you; my stomach was way bigger than that. All my kids gave me a big stomach."

"I guess my baby ain't as big as all your kids."

Felicia took a long drag of her cigarette and Raven turned away and covered her mouth and nose.

"Oh, girl this smoke ain't gonna hurt that baby. Hell, I smoked with all my kids and y'all turned out alright."

Yeah, me and Nia maybe but the rest of them... well, I'll just leave it at that. Raven giggled, grabbing her mother's attention.

"What's funny?"

"Nothing, I was just thinking about something."

"So, what are y'all doing next Saturday?"

Nope, not coming to one of your so-called parties with you and your dope boy as rachet host. "Um, I think I am going to chill with Nia and look for a job."

"Well, y'all need to stop by here. I'm giving my sister-in-law a birthday dinner and I want y'all to be here."

Hell no! "I'll...we'll try. I think we are going to be out all day. I got to start making some money before the baby gets here."

"Hmmm, well, they probably won't care if y'all here or not. I was just trying to be nice."

Raven turned her head again, as her mother inhaled a large puff of her cigarette and exhaled it in her direction; no doubt, it was on purpose. Standing up, she walked to the window and looked out. Nothing but people walking around looking for drugs; kids playing as if they didn't have a care in the world and the dope dealers and addicted people weren't out there in front of them making transactions like their lives depended on it. Police riding by every few minutes. "Why do they even bother to drive by? They not going to do nothing."

"Huh? What was that?"

Raven forgot for a moment that her mother was there, that she was standing in her mother's living room. "Oh...nothing. I was just... nothing."

"I heard your baby daddy left you."

A gasp filled the room followed by shocked silence, which turned to bubbling anger. *Really? Now I see why Nia hate being around her. She don't know what to say out her mouth.*

"I didn't mean to piss you off. I was just saying."

"Nope, you didn't." Pulling out her phone, she tapped her sister's name, her hands shaking the entire time.

I'm ready...

"I got to go..." were the last words she uttered before walking out the door, not bothering to look back nor wait for a reply. Tears began to fall as she reached the bottom of the stairs in the old run down, dusty building. Crackheads lined the stairs along with wads of gum. A string of purple weave laid in the middle of the last step. Blinded for the most part by her tears, she began to feel the sting of being dumped by a boy who she thought loved her; thought care about her. She really didn't have too much emotion about it before, but it was something about the way her mother blurted it out and put it out in the open. It was like it had just become real that Shannon had left her and their child. Finally walking out of the building, she looked at her phone to see if her sister had responded,

On my way...

The tears were fully falling, and she tried her best to wipe them away, ashamed to let anybody see her crying, even though nobody cared. They were all too busy trying to keep their own pain in check.

"It's ok baby. We don't need your father. You don't need somebody like that around you. Somebody who just abandoned you. Trust me, I know." She rubbed her stomach gently and smiled when she felt a slight push. This wasn't the first time she felt movement, but every time felt like Christmas to her. Each time she felt her baby move, it was stronger than the previous time. "Just as long as you got me, you will be ok, and I will never leave you." Two boys whipped past her on dirt bikes and she jumped. "Damn! You would think they would've saw me standing here! Ugh!" Taking slow steady breaths, a technique that the nurse at the clinic taught her to calm herself down, she removed all thoughts from her mind. Focusing on her happy place, as the nurse called it. Her happy place was at the park, with nobody but her and her baby around, surrounded by butterflies and waterfalls.

"Aye!"

Opening her eyes, she saw her sister for the first time sitting in the car, impatiently tooting the horn.

"Girl, what is the matter with you?"

"My bad," Raven answered quickly as she hopped in the car and snapped on her seatbelt.

"She finally pissed you off I see. I knew it was coming one day."

"Yeah, something like that."

"Yep, I know. That's how she is. No filter and don't give a damn about nobody feelings. That's why I don't come over here, but you wanted to see your mother. I tried to tell you."

"Yeah, you did. I'm not coming over here again."

"Good, as you shouldn't."

Looking out the window, Raven looked around and then down at her belly. *Don't worry baby, I'm going to be the best mommy to you. I'll be nothing like your rachet ass grandmother.* Closing her eyes, she allowed her mind to wander back to the place it had before her sister snapped her away from it. Her happy place, where nobody was waiting to tell her how they

told her so or remind her about her issues with
Shannon.

CHAPTER 15

You need to relax! They will call you back in a minute."

Raven looked at Nia and then back at the TV that was on the wall. "We've been in this waiting room all morning. How long does it take to get an ultrasound?"

"I think I remember hearing a lady say that they only one person doing them today, so they are busy. Just chill out."

Raven sighed and rubbed her stomach. *I am dying to know what I'm having.* She closed her eyes and thought of what her baby would look like. She had an ultrasound a few months ago, but all she saw was a bunch of black areas with some alien looking thing on the screen. Chuckling, she remembered asking the nurse was her baby normal; was *she* normal. It was no way that thing could be her baby! "I know you have grown a lot since then," she said and lightly patted her belly. Looking up at the desk and then at the clock on the wall, she sighed. "If they don't hurry up, I'm going to die!"

"If you don't shut up, you're going to die for real! Now sit there and wait."

Raven rolled her eyes at Nia and shifted her weight in the chair. She watched a couple laugh and hug on each other. Looking down at the women's hand, she noticed a big pretty, shiny rock sitting on her finger and she immediately thought of Shannon again for the hundredth time. *Maybe me and Shannon can be like that. Maybe not now, but one day.* Looking at the door, she began to feel a sense of loneliness and sadness. She wished that Shannon would walk through the door, walk through the door so that he could see their baby too; see their baby together. Yea, Nia was ok, but it would be so much better if Shannon was there instead.

"Ms. Mayz!"

Finally. Getting up, Raven smiled at the nurse and turned to look for Nia.

"Go ahead, I'll wait out here."

"You can come back with her."

"Nah, I'm good. I'll just wait out here."

"Oh, come on Nia. I know you don't like stuff like—"

"I sure don't and since you know it already, then why are you still standing there waiting for me to go back with you?"

Raven smacked her lips and proceeded to follow the nurse to the back of the clinic. To her surprise, Nia opened the door and caught up with them. "I'm only doing this because I know how anxious you are, and this is your first baby but I'm not doing this if you have another one."

"K." *I better leave it at that before she changes her mind.*

"Okay, Raven. Go ahead and lay back on the table for me."

Raven grabbed onto the side of the table and slid herself on. The task was so much harder than the first time. She pushed herself up further and slid her shirt up.

"Yep, you got it."

Looking over at Nia, Raven giggled at the look on her face.

"Alright, warm gel."

Raven watched the nurse squeeze the small blue bottle and waited for the warmth to hit her skin. "It feels funny," she said while looking at the screen, waiting impatiently for the nurse to turn on the machine and get started.

"Yeah, it used to be cold until we got the warmer. It would've really felt funny if it was cold," the nurse laughed.

"Yeah," Raven agreed and took a deep breath as the nurse placed the probe on her stomach. Immediately, her eyes lit up at the sight of the well-developed baby that was now on the screen. It looks so much different from before.

"Hmm-hmm," the nurse agreed as she continued to move the probe around.

"Look Nia!"

"I see," Nia said in a tone much softer than her usual one.

"Would you like to know the sex?"

Raven looked at Nia and Nia shrugged her shoulders. She was so anxious before but now that she had the chance to know, she wasn't so sure anymore.

"Yeah, I guess so."

"Okay, do you hope it's a girl or a boy?"

"Um," Raven started. "I would love a little girl so I can dress her up in cute clothes and stuff. But I would be fine with a boy. It really doesn't matter."

"Uh, well, do you have any clothes or anything yet? Any clothes that can be for either a boy or a girl?"

"No, not yet."

The nurse smiled and moved the probe around a bit more. "When you do get some clothes, make sure you get a lot of pink; girls tend to like that color the most."

"A girl!" Raven giggled.

"Yep, a baby girl. Congratulations."

Raven looked over at Nia again and was happy to see the look of happiness spread all over her face.

"Hi little girl. I can't wait until you are here with us. I'm going to be the best mommy in the whole world." Raven smiled so much that her face was beginning to hurt.

"Let me print you off a picture."

"Can you print two?" Raven asked shyly. She looked over at Nia and Nia rolled her eyes. "I want to give one to her father."

"Sure, I can do that."

"Dr. Bass said that she will need a report." Raven said to the nurse but kept her eyes on the screen.

"Yes, I will make sure she gets it. All you have to do is keep that pretty smile on your face and prepare for your little girl."

Raven smiled harder and sat up after the nurse wiped the remaining gel off her stomach. Getting off the table, she watched as the nurse pulled the pictures off the side of the ultrasound machine. She was so giddy that she thought she was going to pass out.

"Here you go."

Raven couldn't take her eyes off the picture of her daughter. "Me and Shannon's baby girl," she whispered before walking out of the exam room and catching up with Nia who had already walked out of the examination room.

CHAPTER 16

"I don't know, I think this one is too white."

Raven laughed. "How can something be *too* white?"

"It just is. I don't want my niece walking around with nothing but white on all the time and then all her sheets are white with no color at all. We need to throw some pink in there somewhere or maybe even green...orange... something."

"Nia, first of all, she won't be walking this early. She is a baby!" Raven playfully yelled.

Nia laughed and pulled more clothes out of the mega sized garbage bag that Jasmine and her mother had brought over for the baby. "Ohhh, this is cute and it's colorful."

"Yeah, that is cute and see, not everything in the bag is white."

"Hmmm," Nia said and proceeded to add it to the color side. We finally got one for this side. Look at all those white clothes over there.

"What is so wrong with white clothes?" Raven laughed. "I think they are nice."

"Yeah nice, but damn. All her baby wore was white and you know babies mess up clothes. So much easier to see when there is no color to hide it."

Raven shook her head at her sister's rant...a rant about nothing. "It was nice of them to bring all these clothes over here. These should last her for a while; at least until she's like one or two." Folding up a blanket that still had the tags on it, she smiled. She thought of what it would be like to wrap her baby up in the blanket. *How does she look? What will her personality be like? And will she be tall or short?* All sorts of questions swarmed her mind. The closer she became to giving birth, the more questions she would think of and the more anxious she was becoming.

"You should probably put that blanket over here in the pile to be washed."

"You sure? It's brand new."

"Yeah, but you still want to wash everything that will touch her. You don't know them like that. So, throw it over here in the laundry pile. Only new stuff that we bought ourselves should be trusted."

"Really Nia," Raven chuckled.

"Yeah girl. You don't know what people do at their house. Just sayin'."

Raven shook her head and threw the blanket over in the laundry pile.

"Chile, y'all look like y'all about to open up a baby shop up in here."

"Hey Aunt Charlotte. My friend Jasmine brought—"

"A girl from school!"

"A friend," Raven corrected her sister and laughed. "A friend of mine from school brought them over. Clothes that her baby had when she was little."

"Oh okay, that was nice of her. That's a lot of nice stuff. I like that dress over there."

The girls looked over at a green and red dress that hung loosely out of the bag. Raven smiled and pulled it out of the pile. "Yeah, it's so cute. Reminds me of Christmas."

"Everything reminds you of Christmas," Nia huffed.

"So," Raven laughed, "what's so wrong with Christmas? That is my favorite holiday."

"Everything don't have to remind you...nevamind chick."

"That's a good dress for her to wear to church. You know I'm going to be coming to get her to take her to church with us"

"Yep, I know." Raven smiled. *Aunt Charlotte and Uncle Charles were the last people I thought I would get help from.* Thoughts of her mother tried to seep in, but she quickly stopped it by reverting to the thoughts of her baby and all the clothes for her that was sitting in front of her. Another technique that her nurse taught her.

"Me and your uncle are going to get you a crib."

"Aww... for real? Thanks Aunt Charlotte."

"You're welcome baby. We were talking about it last night and want to do all we can to help out."

"I really do appreciate that."

"Yeah, dat's was sup Auntie," Nia said while frowning at a shirt, a white shirt.

Raven laughed and shook her head.

"That girl had some nice stuff. Look at this, this is so cute." Charlotte picked up a yellow sundress from the top of the bag and put it in the color pile. "Y'all got the washing detergent yet? You know you can't use what Momma got."

Raven looked at Nia and Nia shrugged her shoulders.

"Why not? What's wrong with that one?"

"A baby's skin is sensitive, so you got to wash all her stuff in a detergent that is made for her type of skin."

"Oh," Raven responded and looked around at all the clothes.

"I'll get you some when I go to the market tonight."

"Okay, thanks." Raven smiled and readjusted herself before her legs started to hurt.

"Hmm-mmm. Well, let me go and get the collards cleaned. Momma want some for Sunday dinner and I got to get em' cleaned before it gets too late." Charlotte smiled at her nieces before she walked out of the room.

"Okay and thank you."

"You're welcome honey. That's what family is for."

"Humph, not all family," Nia said while getting up off the floor. "Somebody needs to tell our sorry, good for nothing ass momma that."

Raven shook her head, moved the piles of clothes over, and put the bag over in the corner. "We'll finish this later. So many clothes, we'll be here all-night sorting them out."

"At least you got some and somebody gave you some. So many people are so selfish these days."

"Yep, you right about that. Ohh, come here and feel!"

"What girl?!"

"Come here before she stops moving!"

"Oh, girl don't be scaring me like that."

Raven smiled as her sister put her hand on her stomach and gasped. "She is so strong, about to kick my hand off."

"I know right! She moves like that all the time."

"Girl, we going to have to get her in sports. That ain't no cheerleader in there; she's a football player the way she in there kicking people."

Raven giggled. "Or maybe a dancer."

"Yeah, a dancer would be—"

"Raven, you got company!"

"Company?" Raven looked over at her phone. 9:12 sat on the screen. "Who would come over here at nine o'clock at night?" She looked at Nia and Nia looked out the window.

"I don't know? I don't see... wait, I know that is not who I think it is."

Raven's intuition sparked and she joined her sister at the window. A mop of black hair that illuminated from the porch light was seen first, followed by the look of sorrow etched across his face as he impatiently looked around. Raven gasped and placed her hand on her stomach. "How does he even know I'm here?"

"Who cares? Let's just go and cuss his ass out!"

Nia hastily walked away from the window and out of her room.

"Nia! No!" Raven yelled as she chased her sister down before she had a chance to reach the front door. *He done me dirty, but I still love him, and he is my baby's father.* Finally reaching the bottom of the stairs, she saw the face that she was longing to see for months. Shannon stood on the front porch, in her eyes, looking as fine as ever.

"Why are you here?!"

"Uh–uh Nia! Leave that alone!"

"Nah Auntie! That dude just goin' leave my sister at the drop of a dime and then goin' bring his—"

"Get in here!"

Raven watched as her aunt pulled her sister into the house and closed the door, leaving Shannon out on the front porch.

"Raven go on out there and talk to him. I got your sister."

"Somebody should smack his ass!"

"Alright! Now! Watch your mouth girl!"

"Yeah fo' I pop yo' mouth."

"Grandma—"

"Hush! And go somewhere and sat down before I knock you down!"

"It's *sit* down, Grandma," Nia said, risking a slap from her no-nonsense grandmother.

Raven looked at the door but couldn't move. She wasn't sure on what she was going to say to him; a boy who blatantly just walked away from her and their child and didn't bother to look back. *All these months and now, he's back.*

"Raven?"

Looking at her aunt, she sighed, knowing what the next question would be and then all her time to stall would be out the window.

"I'm going," she answered quickly and opened the door. A small breeze blew as she opened the storm door. The quiver that she felt so many times before when she saw him was still there but this time, it was magnified by ten. She put her right hand on her stomach, hoping that she would see something in Shannon's eyes. "Nothing," she mumbled.

"You should probably go get a jacket or something. I think it's about to rain." Shannon mumbled.

"I'm good." She watched his eyes as they moved down to her belly and she smirked. *At least he finally looked at it. I know he couldn't be that careless.* A slow and steady breeze filled the space, but Raven still felt incredibly hot. She wasn't quite sure if it was hormones, nervousness, or Shannon that caused her feelings, but she knew one of them had to start talking and since he came to her, then it should be him.

"So…"

He looked around and then back at her. "How you doing?"

"Don't you mean we? How are *we* doing? We are fine except for the fact that you dumped me like I am some random hoe off the streets and like she is somebody else's." She pointed to her belly for emphasis.

"She?"

Raven softened her tone at the fact that Shannon softened his attitude about the situation. "Yes, it's a girl. Our daughter; our baby girl."

"Yo, I'm sorry about how everything went down. My moms be acting funny like that when she feels like things are falling apart around here. It's something she does; nothing against you...or the baby."

"Your baby. And I can't tell that she doesn't have a problem with me or our baby."

The warm and tingling feeling was gone, and the cool air began to wrap Raven around in its grips as if she was in a deep, walk in freezer. It was June so it really wasn't cold out but to Raven, it seemed like they were in January. Wrapping her arms around her shoulders, she shivered.

"You ok? You cold?"

"Yep, that's what anemia will do to you; make you feel so cold when everybody else around you is comfortable. Pregnancy induced anemia is what the doctor called it."

"Oh, but you and the baby are alright though. Right?"

"Yeah, I just have to take an iron pill every day, but we are good. I take it when I take my prenatal vitamins."

"Oh, dats was sup."

Raven shifted herself and leaned on the railing. "So, how did you know I was here?"

"Oh, um, your aunt told me. I went over there to see you and she told me that you had moved over here to your grandma's house."

"Oh. Yeah, I had to get out of there. I like it so much better over here. Now that it's summertime, I don't have to worry about catching the bus all the way to school."

"Yeah," Shannon said while pacing slightly. Maybe you can get a cheap car or something or your sister can take you to school next year."

"Yeah, maybe. Or you can just take us. I signed up for the daycare at school so I will be taking the baby with me on school days. My aunt is going to watch her while I work at night so it will be better if you do it so I

185

can have time enough to get ready for work and then take her to my Aunt Charlotte's house."

Raven frowned slightly at Shannon, wondering why he wasn't saying anything and looking down at the porch steps. "Um, everything ok? Why you get all quiet on me?"

"Huh? Oh, nothing. I was just thinking of another way that you could get to school. I'm not going to be able to that. Maybe I can help you get—"

"Why?"

"Why... what?"

Raven began to feel the warm feeling that she'd felt when she first walked out on the porch but this time, she was sure that it was anger. Something about the look on his face and the intuition that was calling out to her told her that something was wrong; that he wasn't over there to get back together and live the family life.

"Why can't you take us?" She repeated. "You work at night so it shouldn't be a problem."

"Raven," he sighed. "I just came to check on you and that's it. I'm not tryin' to get back with you or nothing, but I will take care of the baby."

"What?" She said in a hoarse whisper. She felt tears forming but she worked as hard as she could to keep them within her tear ducts. She gripped her belly, hoping that would change his mind but he continued with his *why I can't be with you* speech.

"I-my girl—"

"Your girl?"

"Look Raven, I'm trying to man up and do right by my kid. Don't make this harder than it has to be."

At that very moment, Raven felt the sting that all the old love and blues songs were singing about. At sixteen, she now knows what it felt like to be pregnant, to love someone so much more than she loved herself, the feeling of neglect by someone who was supposed to love her unconditionally, and now, the awful ache of a broken heart.

"I will do everything that I can to make sure that the baby is well taken care of and so will my mom. She ain't trippin' no more now that I told her the truth. I know that's my—"

Raven put her left hand up and covered her mouth with her right, feeling an overwhelming feeling of nausea and dizziness.

"Yo, you alright?"

Working as hard as she could to get herself together, Raven wiped her face, looked over, and held on to the side railing to steady herself. "I can't believe you."

"What?"

"What? What do you mean what? Since when do you have another girlfriend?"

"Look, I..."

Suddenly, the faint sound of music came from the direction of Shannon's truck.

"Who is that in the... did you bring another girl to my house?!"

"Yo chill, it's just my girl and she—"

"Oh, I cannot believe you!" Pushing Shannon, Raven leapt off the porch, jogged over to Shannon's truck, and ripped open the passenger seat. What she saw next had her feeling like she was for sure going to pass out; nothing like the small bouts of dizziness she'd been feeling. This was a whole new level of dizziness and lightheadedness. Carla! Yep, as in her sister Carla, stared back at her but instead of the frown that was usually plastered on her face, she had a big grin, showing off braces with red brackets that nobody in the family knew she had.

CHAPTER 17

I still can't believe that," Raven whispered quietly to herself while she gazed out the window at her grandmother's clothesline. *"My sister? Out of all the girls in the world, all the girls in Baltimore, he had to choose my sister. I guess it helps that he didn't know she was my sister, but she did, and I know she knew exactly what she was doing too. Acting just like Ma; doing me dirty the same way Ma did Aunt Joyce way back in the day. Even if she didn't know when they first got together, she knew where she was when they got over here to grandma's house."*

"What's got you so quiet over the past few days?"

Nia hopped on her bed and tossed a pillow at Raven. "Ever since that dog you call your man—"

Raven turned to her sister in a sharp twist and rolled her eyes at her.

"My bad, I meant your baby daddy. Either way, he ain't no good. You were so pissed off when you came back in the house the other night. What happened?"

Raven sighed and closed the curtains. *Should I say something...Nah, I kept it to myself this long; I can just not say anything. I can't tell people that my boyfriend dumped me for my sister; my triflin' sister who has a nasty attitude with everybody. I can't tell nobody nothing that embarrassing, even if it is Nia.* "Nothing, just a lot—"

"Oh, girl stop! This is me you're talking to. What happened with Shannon? I know it's him that got you all quiet."

Tears began to well up in Raven's eye and was moving too fast to catch them before they tricked down her face.

"Raven..."

Raven turned to herself as the tears began to move faster. All the tears that she'd been storing up was now out and it was nothing that she could do about it.

"What happened?"

Raven wiped her eyes, but the tears continued to fall.

"Raven!"

"Carla..." Sitting down on the floor, she slid her knees up under her stomach in an attempt to tuck them under her, a position she would get into when she was feeling uncomfortable and needed to calm down, but quickly slid them out instead when she felt the weight of her pregnant belly.

"Carla? What about Carla?"

The sight of her sister sitting in Shannon's truck brought on more tears and a few hiccups.

"Girl! What about—?"

"She is messing with Shannon!"

Raven kept her head down, knowing that Nia was getting ready to go off but there was a long period of silence instead. She looked up to see her sister in a state of rage. Yes, she was quiet, but the look of hatred was plastered all over her face.

"Nia?"

In an instant, Nia jumped up and stormed out of her room.

Raven tried to stand up, but her legs were as numb and as rubbery as one of those old school rubber chickens. Vigorously rubbing her legs, the numbness subsided, and she was able to stand up. Standing up too fast, she was dizzy and nauseous but after taking some slow deep breaths, she began to feel normal again. Just in time to hear Nia's car door slam. "Nia! Damn it!" *I know she is on her way over to Aunt Charlotte's house.* "Nia! Shoot!" Rushing down the stairs as fast as she could, she slipped on one of the steps. "Ow!" She yelled and sat down.

"What is going on with y'all?" her grandmother called out towards the stairs. "And where is Nia going?"

"Grandma tell Nia to wait!"

"What in the world is going—?"

"Grandma," she said in a lighter tone, stopping herself from getting slapped in the mouth, a gesture that she was known for no matter your age or your condition. "Can you please tell Nia to stop? I want to ride."

"Okay but where y'all going?"

"To the store," she blurted out. The first thing that came to mind.

She rubbed her left ankle and patted her pants pocket for her phone. "Damn, I left it up... Nia!" She yelled when Nia ran back into the house and up the stairs, running right past her.

"Nia!"

Nia walked out of her room, stuffing something in her pocket.

"Nia, wait for me!"

She didn't have to ask where she was going because her movements and the *pissed off bitch* look on her face told it all. Raven just wanted to be there to watch the butt whippin' go down. Standing up, she walked up the stairs and quickly decided to leave her phone and follow Nia to her car instead.

"Y'all bring back some corn meal from the store. I want to cook some—"

"Okay Grandma, we gotchu'", Raven said while swiftly pulling her lemonade braids up in a ponytail and pushing her feet in her sister's flip flops before rushing out the door and sliding into the passenger seat. Without saying another word, she held onto the side of the door handle as Nia drove like a bat out of hell to find their backstabbing sister.

"Paradise," Raven mumbled while looking at all the big beautiful houses that lined her aunt Charlotte and uncle Charles' street. *Out of all my mom's kids, Carla was the lucky one to move in with the rich side of the family. Then have to be the one that is the most ungrateful.*

"I can't believe that bitch." Nia hissed.

Raven looked over at Nia. The same look of hatred and fire was still all over her face.

"How she gonna mess with somebody her sister had? I know she crazy and all but damn, that's messed up."

Raven felt a sense of satisfaction. Since she couldn't fight Carla, she was glad that she had Nia to do it for her. She was so mad at Carla that she thought she'd seen the devil himself in the truck with her the night she found out about her and Shannon. *I should've told Nia when it first happened. I knew that she wouldn't look at me as weak. I had nothing to be embarrassed about. It's your own fault.* Raven put her head down as her conscious whispered to her. *You should've made sure Shannon knew all your sisters instead of trying to hide the fact that you have so many.*

194

The car stopped, causing a feeling of high and a feeling of dread within Raven's body both moving around all at the same time. Nia jumped out of the car and jogged up the driveway and to the side door. Raven tried to get out just as fast, but the throbbing of her ankle was slowing her down. "Damn," she huffed. She watched Nia walk into the house and her uncle wave at her. She waved back and used all her strength to get out of the car. Pain shot up her leg, but she ignored it and walked as quickly as she could.

"Hey baby. Look likes you got a big one in there."

"How you doing, Uncle Charles?"

"Yeah, looks like..."

"You are a slutty hoe!"

Both Raven and her uncle turned towards the commotion that was going on up the stairs.

"What is happening with—?"

A big boom followed by the sound of glass shattering startled them both and Charles jogged towards the stairs, leaving a slow and injured Raven behind.

"Let her go!" Charlotte yelled.

"Charlotte! What is going on?" Charles yelled towards the stairs.

"Charles! Get up here and get these girls!"

"Lord have mercy!" Charlotte hollered.

Another round of booms and bangs took over the noise of the TV playing in the living room. Raven moved slowly up the stairs while Charles jogged. Finally reaching Carla's bedroom, Raven smiled internally at the sight of Carla getting her butt beat. A well-deserved butt whippin' in her eyes and Nia was for sure handling business. She didn't want her aunt nor her uncle to see just how happy she was at the fact that Carla was getting a beat down.

"Aye! Stop!" Charles yelled and pulled Nia off Carla. Spots of blood was on Carla's face and Raven smirked. *The same tears that were on mine, blood is on yours. That's what you get.*

"Calm down! What are y'all fighting for?!" Charles asked with a deep frown on his face.

"What is this all about?" Charlotte joined in.

"That hoe is messing with Raven's boyfriend!"

Charlotte looked at Carla and then at Raven. "Shannon?" She asked in a voice full of uncertainty.

Raven looked at her aunt and a fresh set of tears began to form. "You know him?"

"Yeah, Carla... oh Lord. Honey, I am so sorry."

"Carla, did you know that Shannon is—?"

"He don't mess wit' her like dat no more."

Nia lunged at Carla, but Charles grabbed her before she could reach her target.

"Girl! What is the matter with you?!" Charlotte frowned. "See, that's the kind of mess your momma used to do. Messed around with Joyce husband and that's why they can't stand each other. Why you gotta' be like her?"

"He don't want nobody with a baby! So, I got with him."

Raven balled her fist as her blood was beginning to boil. The sight of her sister made her sick and she was ready to smack that smile off her face. Taking slow deep breaths, she held her stomach instead and continued to stay quiet.

"Girl, that ain't got nothing to do with you! So, you knew who Shannon was in the first place. You knew that he was your niece's father and you still brought him over to the house like you met him fair and square."

"That's foul little girl," Charles said while still holding Nia. "That's just foul."

A renewed strength placed itself within Raven at the family support. Her family understood just how wrong Carla was for messing around with Shannon.

"Does Shannon know that you and Raven are sisters?" Charlotte asked with a look of concern spread across her face.

All eyes fell on bloody-faced Carla as they waited for a response.

"I don't be going around tellin' people that she is my sister. That none of them is my sisters."

"Good! Cause we don't like yo' ass anyway!" Nia yelled.

"Aye!"

Nia glanced at Charles and then hastily looked back at Carla. Carla rolled her eyes and wiped her lip.

"Go and get you a tissue or something to wipe your lip. The first aid kit is in the medicine cabinet. Bring it here."

Nia nudged Charles as Carla walked past. "I hate her!" She yelled.

"Hey! Stop all that! It's over now; you handled it so it's time to chill out now," Charles said as he lightly loosened his grip.

"Let me go, Uncle Charles," Nia responded instead of agreeing with him.

"Not until I know you ain't gonna jump on that girl. You already kicked her—"

"Charles... no."

"No what? Well, she did."

Charlotte shook her head and walked over to Raven.

Raven leaned against the wall as pain from her ankle shot through her calf. "Ow," she winced and rubbed it gently, noticing a small lump on the side of it.

"That ankle is sprained, chile."

"Nah, I think it's just bruised a little."

"I have been a nurse for over thirty years; I'm telling you, it's sprained. Put a little ice on it to bring the swelling down and keep it elevated on some pillows for a few days."

Raven continued to rub her ankle, not bothering to give any attention to Carla that had walked into the room and rolled her eyes.

"Why do you keep coming in here where you got your—?"

"Charles!"

"Charles, what? She did."

"Bitch," Nia said before wiggling her way out of Charles' grip and walking out of the room and down the stairs.

Raven moved off the wall and followed behind her. *So, he didn't know.* A glimmer of hope crept into her mind; hope that she, her man, and their baby could actually live happily ever after. *Hmmm, maybe I can be a nurse like Aunt Charlotte and Shannon can be an architect in the Army just like Uncle Charles. He's already in the Army Reserves, it'll be easy for him to transition so we can have a house like this.* Raven looked around at the elegant paintings that draped all over the walls throughout the house. The different color paint that matched perfectly with the furniture in each room caught her attention and she smiled. *Yeah, a life like this.* She glanced over at the huge fireplace and a big picture of her aunt Charlotte in her wedding gown that sat above it in the living room. *Yep, that could be me in my wedding... well, I won't take it that far. Maybe just—*

"Come on Raven, let's go!" Nia yelled, clearly still mad.

Moving her thoughts off to the side, Raven hugged her aunt and uncle before joining her sister outside. She took one last look at her dream house before getting in the car. A dream that can possibly become reality now that she knew the truth about Shannon and Carla.

CHAPTER 18

R aven opened her eyes to the sun shining brightly in her face. Yawning, she looked down at her own personal basketball; a small sized basketball due to her baby's low weight and not quite growing appropriately for her gestational age.

"Good morning my little Miracle. Good morning," she whispered and rubbed her belly gently, waiting to feel movement. "Right on time," she cooed as she felt a small kick.

"Why are you still sitting there and not dressed? You know we have to be at Aunt Charlotte's house in like an hour."

"I was up late studying for my math test."

"Why? You getting ready to go on maternity leave. Why are you still studying?"

"Uh, because I want to pass so I can go to college. Just because I'm getting ready to leave out for a while, doesn't mean that I don't have responsibilities."

"Ohhh, look at you. Sounding all like a mother."

"Shut up," Raven laughed and stood up.

"I can't wait to see all of Miracle's stuff. I know Aunt Charlotte invited all her nurse and doctor friends, so she is getting ready to get some pretty stuff."

"Yeah, she sure is. Did you invite her family?"

"Please. What family? All her family is right here, the way they been acting."

"You know Aunt Charlotte, she probably invited them. At least Shannon's mother."

Raven waved her hand and walked out of the room. The smell of bacon and coffee met her, and she smiled. "Grandma got it smellin' all good up in here this morning."

"You know how she is. As soon as it starts getting cold outside, she gets in the mood for bacon and coffee."

Raven laughed at the look on Nia's face, a look of disgust. "Yeah, I know you hate coffee and bacon."

"Who hates bacon?"

"Girl bye, you know I don't eat that stuff."

"Y'all better come on. Charlotte called and said we need to be going."

"Okay!" Raven called down to her grandmother, grabbed a towel and wash cloth from the hall closet, and went into the bathroom.

"You got it set up so nice, Charlotte."

Charlotte put the cake on the table and placed the gift bag that her friend Ingrid brought and placed it on the gifts table. "Thanks Ingrid, I wanted to do something nice for Raven. The poor girl has been through so much over the past few months."

"Yeah, finding out that her baby isn't growing like they had hoped and dealing with all the stuff from her momma. How is she doing?"

"Chile, she is just happy that the baby wasn't born early and that the doctors were able to stop her labor. She started having pains the other night and had to go to the hospital. They told her that she has to stop being stressed out over all the stuff going on. I've been telling her that, but you know teenagers chile, they don't listen."

"Right, it's the same way with my granddaughter, Erica. Don't think I know what I'm talking about." Ingrid shook her head.

"Oh, I know chile."

"You sure you don't need me to do anything, Charlotte?"

"Oh no, I got it. I think we got everything set. My niece Nia is going to do all the games so just waiting for her, Raven, and momma to get here. I invited Felicia but that thang said she couldn't come. Something about her man is in jail and she got to get him out or some mess."

"Stop!"

"Yep, I washed my hands of it all. I don't know what goes on in that girl head, chile. I just try to do right for her daughters; all five of them."

Ingrid shook her head and repositioned herself in her seat.

"Even that little grownish one she got. I try to do for her too. Even though her momma spoils her and the one who she loves to death, I still try to help out with her."

"Well, that's the right thing to do; the Christian thing to do."

"Yep, that's right. I heard Felicia is back on those drugs." Charlotte said while moving the party contents around on the table.

"Girl stop!"

"Hmm, yes chile. I haven't said anything to Charles or Momma so keep it to yourself."

"Oh, my goodness. She still ain't learned her lesson from the last time? When she overdosed on that stuff?"

"Chile, she..."

"Hey!" A handful of Charlotte's relatives walked in, stopping her tea from spilling over with her friend.

"Hey y'all! Thank y'all for coming."

"You know we had to be here. You got it decked out so nice in here." Marjorie, Charlotte's oldest sister said and smiled.

"Yeah, I wanted to do something nice for Raven. She got so much going on. Y'all get y'all some cookies. They in there on the table. Nia texted and said they were on the way so they should be here soon."

"Marjorie, that wrapping paper is so pretty. Put it over there on the gift table. That is a pretty purple."

"Thank you. I had it left over from my grandbaby's baby shower, so I just used the rest of that paper."

"They should be here any minute. Girl, I been cooking for seem like days; started yesterday."

"Do you need me to do anything?" Marjorie asked.

"No, I think I got everything under control. I've been... here they come pulling up now. Okay y'all let's go on in the living room. They are here now!"

"Hey! Y'all come on in." Charlotte opened the door and yelled.

Raven got out of the backseat and opened the passenger side door for her grandmother. She looked around at the decorations that lined the porch and smiled gleefully. *All this is for me. All this is for Miracle. Something is finally done for me and it's all mine.* She looked past Charlotte in the doorway and saw people moving around. *They are all in there waiting for me and my baby.* Smiling harder, she held onto her grandmother's hand while Nia pulled her cane out of the trunk.

"Come on Grandma, I got your cane."

Raven helped her grandmother maneuver out of the seat and to her cane. All the while, thinking of how good it felt finally to have people paying attention to her. She didn't have to fight for it like she did with her mother. On this day, she didn't have to wonder why she wasn't liked by her aunt Joyce, well, unless it benefited her in some way. This time, people were waiting to surround her and to shower her and the one person she knew would love her no matter what, with love and gifts. *And it ain't even Christmas*, she gleamed.

"You got it Momma?"

"Yeah, I'm making it."

Raven walked beside her grandmother, wishing that she could speed up so they could all hurry up and get to celebrating her.

"You got it so pretty."

"Thank you, Momma. Come on in here and let me get you something to drink."

"Yeah, cause my mouth is dry."

"Nia, come on in here and get your grandmother some lemonade."

"You want lemonade Momma or some water?"

"Lemonade. You know I don't want no water."

Raven waited for her grandmother to make it up the last step and walk into the house before she stepped in. The inside was decorated more beautiful than the outside and Raven gushed with happiness.

"How are you feeling today, Raven? The baby doing ok?"

"I'm feeling good and the baby is ok too. Thank you, Aunt Charlotte," she beamed and gave her aunt a hug.

"You're welcome baby. Glad to do it for you."

"How y'all doing?"

Raven, Nia, and her grandmother exchanged pleasantries with the guests and sat down in the living room. Raven continued to look around in awe at all the decorations and all the gifts that were on the pink and yellow table. She spotted a diaper cake on the table next to a big box of wipes. "That is so pretty!"

"I'm glad you like it honey."

"That's my friend Ingrid." Charlotte said while moving some chairs around. "She can make those things chile."

Raven smiled, "Thank you so much for making it for me."

"You're welcome. I like making them, so I'll make you a few more, in different colors before you go in."

"Okay!"

"You got it lit up in here Aunt..." Nia stopped as she gazed out the window.

Raven looked up at Nia and frowned. "What?"

The rest of the guest looked towards Nia's gaze.

"What is it?" Raven asked again and stood up.

"Nothing. I just see your baby daddy and his momma walking up."

"Huh?"

"I hope you don't mind sweetie. I called Shannon's mom and she really wanted to come."

"How did you get her phone...? Oh yeah, Carla."

Nia's face changed from surprise to anger in a matter of seconds. The mention of Carla's name caused a big change in attitudes. Not just from Nia but from everybody in the family.

"That girl ain't here is she?" Nia asked through clenched teeth.

"No, I sent her to the little day camp that the church does on Saturdays. She will be there all day today." Charlotte answered.

"Oh, that's where she needs to be...right there in church," Nia replied.

Raven kept her eyes on the door. Beginning to feel a bit anxious, she stood up to go to the bathroom but by the time she turned, Shannon and his mom were standing at the door, looking just as uncomfortable as she was feeling.

"Hi! Come on in!"

Raven sat back down in the chair and smiled. *It's time to act right.* "Hi, thank y'all for coming," she said quickly and grabbed one of the yellow napkins that sat on the coffee table.

"Hey Raven. It's nice to see you again." Shannon's mother walked over quickly to Raven and stood beside her.

"Raven?"

Looking over at her aunt, she frowned and then looked up at Shannon's mom. "Oh," she muttered before she stood up to give Shannon's mom a quick hug. She then walked over to Shannon and gave him a church hug before walking back to her seat and sitting down.

"Please have a seat," Charlotte said and pointed her hand towards the couch.

"Shannon, let me get you a chair so you can sit next to Raven."

"Uh, okay."

Shannon caught a glimpse of his mom's scowl. "I can get the chair," he said quickly. "Is one from the kitchen ok?" He looked back at his mom for approval. She turned away so he continued. "This one?"

"Yep, that'll work," Charlotte said while walking into the kitchen.

"Raven, did you see the cake?" Charlotte smiled.

"No ma'am, not yet."

Raven was nervous but yet so happy at the same time. Shannon was sitting with her and their baby, being a part of it all. *This is the best day of my life. I can't believe Shannon and his mom are here with us; helping us get ready for our baby.*

"Okay! Let's get this party started!" Charlotte yelled.

"Momma, do you need to go to the bathroom or anything before we start the games?"

No, I'm alright for right now.

"Okay."

"Raven, do you want to run in there and see the cake real quick before we start?"

Raven looked at Shannon and then at her Aunt Charlotte. "Okay."

"Alright, go take a look and let me know what you think while Nia gets the first game ready."

"Nia, you got the pens? I got the..."

Raven got up and walked towards the kitchen, turning, she motioned for Shannon to follow her. "Aww," she said and put her hand over her mouth in surprise and pure bliss. The cake was two tiers, decorated with a pair of pink and white baby shoes on the top tier and ribbons and bows all over the bottom one. "That is so pretty." She looked over at Shannon and was happy to see a smile on his face.

"Yeah, it is," he answered and moved closer to Raven. Shannon looked and began to seem a little more comfortable than when he first arrived. Raven continued to admire the cake, thinking of something to say to keep the conversation going for as long as she could. She put her hand on her belly and looked at Shannon. "Um, I want to thank you for coming."

"Oh, um, no problem. Glad your aunt invited me," he smiled and touched Raven's cheek.

Raven began to blush, and Miracle began to move.

"Do you want to feel? She moves around a lot."

Shannon backed away a little and licked his lips. "I don't know. I..."

Raven grabbed Shannon's hand and put it on her stomach, not bothering to wait for his excuse on why it wouldn't be a good idea.

He abruptly moved back when the baby kicked.

Raven laughed. "It's ok, she's just saying hello."

"She kicks hard," Shannon chuckled. "Does it hurt?"

"No, most of the time it doesn't but, she has been known to kick me hard enough to wake me up at night."

Raven and Shannon both laughed.

"Dat's was sup," he said and leaned against the counter. "You know Raven, I'm sorry for—"

"Shhh, all that is old news. Let's just focus on now and Miracle."

"Miracle?"

"Yeah, that's her... I'm sorry, I never told you her name. You fell back and we weren't—"

"It's all good; I like it. Miracle Shahad. Yeah, I like that."

"Shahad?" *Oh, hell no, I wasn't planning on giving her your last name.* "Yeah," she said instead. Miracle Shahad."

"Alright, we are all ready for the games!"

Raven and Shannon both looked at each other and then walked into the living room.

"Okay, Shannon, you go ahead and sit down."

"Raven you stand in the center over there. We are going to guess the size of—"

"Oh, no Aunt Charlotte, we decided to take that one out."

Raven was glad that Nia had spoken up for her. With Miracle's condition, they both decided last minute to remove the "size of the belly" tissue game. She didn't want to be judged for having a smaller sized baby. They were already talking about her age all of the time. No need to give them more to gossip about.

"Oh, okay baby. Well, let's play the word scramble. Everybody grab a pen and one of the papers off the—"

"I know she is not coming up in here!" Nia yelled, abruptly cutting her aunt off.

Raven frowned and walked over to the window. She huffed when she was her mother walking quickly towards the house.

"Aunt Charlotte, did you—?"

"Nah, I didn't invite her, so I don't know why she's here. I don't even know how she knows about it."

Charlotte hurried to the door and stepped outside on the porch. Nia and Raven both kept frowns on their faces while their mother and their aunt had it out on the porch.

"Lord have mercy. Now why that girl come all the way over here to start some mess?"

"Cause she crazy Grandma, that's why," Nia hastily answered her grandmother and walked to the door.

"Girl don't you go out there! Come back here!"

Nia ignored her grandmother and stood at the door. Raven sat down on the couch and put her head down.

"You ok?" Shannon whispered.

"Yeah, I'm good. Just tired of her and her mess." She looked over at Shannon's mother, hoping that she didn't think the worst about her family, about her granddaughter's family. This was the one moment she had to prove to the Shahad family that she and her family were just as normal as they were. *Ma had to come along and ruin it.*

"Can I get anybody anything to drink?" Ingrid asked.

Everyone all said no and kept their attention on the argument that was going on outside.

"Thanks for asking Ms. Ingrid," Raven smiled. Hoping that would somehow lighten the mood.

"Why are you even here?!"

"Uh oh, Nia is all in it now," Raven mumbled as she jumped up from the chair.

"Come on Nia, she's not worth the time." Raven said as she walked up to the door.

"Oh, so you got something against me coming to your shower too, huh?"

Raven blinked her eyes and turned away, working hard to keep her composure. With all the hormones running through her body, she could either break down and cry at any given moment or go off in a hell storm, ready to fight anybody in sight. Knowing that she had her daughter to protect, she breathed through her anger and consciously went for the first reaction. *At least a few tears will get me some sympathy, especially from Shannon.* She closed her eyes and listened to her aunt, sister, and mother argue. Pulling from their emotion, she tried to bring the tears, but nothing would fall. Anger was clearly winning the battle; no matter how hard she tried to move it out of her. It was there and it was strong.

"Move! I got something to say!"

"Felicia... girl... Get out of my house!"

"Nope, not until I say what I have to say! Y'all claimed y'all was helping me with my kids and y'all ain't done nothing but stir them all in the wrong direction. Got them having babies and shit!"

"Hey! Now I don't want you in here but since you barged your way in, you are going to watch your mouth!"

"Charlotte, let me say what I have to say and then I will leave your house!"

"Y'all all sitting around like y'all are better parents than me. Ain't none of y'all no better than me!"

"Girl you better go ahead and say what you got to say so you can get out of here! Don't make me smack you!"

"Momma, I'm going to go. I just came to ask one question."

Raven watched as her mother looked at Shannon and then at Shannon's mother. "Where y'all from?"

"Oh my gosh," Raven sighed and put her head in her hands.

"Excuse me?"

"I asked a simple question. Where are y'all from? Y'all clearly ain't from this country so where y'all—"

"Felicia, go ahead and say what it is you want to say so you can get out of my house!"

Now that Raven didn't want to cry, she just wanted this whole thing to be over, the tears were building up and ready to fall. Whether she wanted them to or not, they were taking their place in her eyes and getting ready to fall at any minute.

"Okay! Fine! Momma, if I'm such a bad mother, why is my child getting pregnant on purpose?!"

Raven gasped as the living room began to spin around in circles and her head was getting ready to explode. Nausea was at its worst and low back pain was forming at the lowest part of her spine.

"What?" Shannon asked in a hoarse whisper. "Yo, what is she talking about?"

"Tell him Raven. Tell him how you planned all this so you could trap him."

"Damn it!" Shannon yelled before getting up and storming out, his mother right behind him.

"Shannon! I didn't do...Come back!"

"What the hell is wrong with you?!" Nia spat at her mother.

"Mind your business Nia!"

"Raven, no baby... No."

Raven looked up at her Aunt Charlotte and put her head down. "I just wanted to be loved," she muttered. "I needed something or somebody to love. I didn't do it to trap him. I just—"

"Lord have mercy, girl."

Raven put her attention on her grandmother and put her head down at the look of disappointment plastered on her face.

"Either way, you ruined that boy's life! Something is wrong with you!"

"Well if it is, then I learned it from you!" Raven yelled at her mother.

Nia walked over to Raven and put her arms around her. "Don't worry about her, I got her. You just stay calm."

How the hell did she find out I did it on...
purpose. Raven wiped her eyes and thought as hard as she could. A glimpse of Shannon's truck came into view as he sped off. Moving thoughts of him off her mind, she focused on the question at hand. *How did she know what I did?* All the arguing and bickering became a blur as she used all of her brainpower to try to figure out how her secret got out. *Maybe it was... that damn Carla. Of course, that's who it was. That bitch who's just as sneaky and conniving as she is. Yeah, she had to be the one to tell her. But how did she know?*

"Well, maybe if you were there for the girl and acted like a real mother to her, then she might not be in this situation!"

"That's it, Charlotte; blame it all on me!"

"You are the reason a lot of stuff happens," Nia joined in. "I can remember times when I wanted to do things because I felt like nobody didn't care about me but then grandma stepped in. If it wasn't for her, I don't know where I would be. You dump Raven on Aunt Joyce! Out of all the people you could've sent her to, you pick the one who hates you and because of what you did, she hates all of us."

In quick minute, a bell went off in Raven's head and she gasped. *When I was going over my calendar, her and Aunt Charlotte was at Aunt Joyce house. It was Carla. Yep, that's exactly what happened. That bitch got my calendar book and was reading my stuff.*

"Who told you?!"

Everyone turned their attention on Raven and Raven kept the perfect frown on her face.

"Why does that matter?"

"I have a right to know who told my business!"

"You're only sixteen lil' girl, you don't have any business."

Raven felt like she was about ready to burst open. Literally, pop open and break in half she was so mad.

"I got more *real* business than you got!"

"Lil girl, don't make me smack—"

"And when you do, be ready for the same kind of ass whippin' your daughter got!" Nia yelled.

"Nia! I told you to mind your business!"

"And I told you and still telling you that I will put these hands on you! Don't try me!"

"Nia! Don't you talk to yo' momma like that! She is still your—"

"She ain't no mother of mine Grandma! That trick can go somewhere and take several seats! The only child she got is that spoiled ass little girl who live with her and her drug dealer daddy."

"Okay! Alright! That's enough!" Charlotte yelled.

Everybody in the room got quiet and Raven put her head down. *This is not happening. That lady did not just break up my happiness and my family in a matter of minutes; something that took me months to build. I try to be better than her and she takes it from me. Just like that.*

"I want to thank all of you for coming. Anybody want some cake? At least get a piece of cake before y'all go."

Raven heard her Aunt Charlotte's voice, but it sounded blurred. Her mind was consumed with thoughts of the life that she was so close to having and her mother ruined it all for her. She thought of a way to get back at her, but her mind drew a blank. Yeah, her mother was rude and vindictive, but she was not; there was nothing popping up in her mind that would cause her mother the same pain that she was in. *I must get this kind-heartedness from my daddy, whoever that is.* Her eyes filled with hatred and tears as she looked at her mother. The crooked smile on her face taunted her but still, she couldn't think of a single thing or one action that would destroy her. Give her the same, if not worse, pain that she was feeling.

"Felicia, why? Why would you come in here and do that? Come in here in front of everybody and say the things you said?"

Raven looked around the now empty room with the exception of family and then at her mother, waiting for her to answer her Aunt Charlotte's question.

"Cause she's a bitch! That's why!"

"Nia! Now I done told you to watch your mouth! Go on in the kitchen, pack up the rest of the cake, and take it to the car. Then you can come back and get the gifts. Go on before Momma smacks you in the mouth." Charlotte said as she placed her hands on her hips.

"I sure am if she don't stop."

Nia and Raven both looked at their grandmother. Nia mumbled something under her breath and walked out of the living room. Grabbing her stomach, Raven looked at her mother and shook her head. If there was any love before, there sure wasn't any now.

"I don't think it's right for a sixteen-year-old girl to be planning pregnancies and stuff. That's why I said something."

"Yeah but you didn't have to say it now! Today?! In front of everybody."

"You! Are you serious right now?"

"Raven, honey, don't get yourself all—" Charlotte started before Raven yelled out.

"You! The worst mother in the world have the nerve to stand there and say that I shouldn't be planning nothing. Well, at least I'm woman enough to take care of my baby. I'm not going to throw her away and give her to family to raise so I can go out and get high all day and all night! You are the worst mother ever so don't come up in here telling my business and messing up what I got."

"Humph, looks like I did that already."

In an instant, Raven hopped up and lunged at her mother. Charlotte ran and jumped in front of Raven before she could reach her target. "No baby! That ain't the way to handle this."

"Nia! Come and take Raven out to the car."

Raven was so mad that she was shaking all over. She allowed Nia to take her hand and walk her to the car.

"Don't worry about her. You can beat her ass after you have the baby. Don't be risking Miracle's life over that!" Nia looked at Felicia and rolled her eyes. "She ain't worth it."

"And neither is you! Y'all ain't no daughters of mine. I got my daughter and she's at home with her daddy."

Raven tried her hardest to ignore her and to not allow her emotions to get the best of her, but the tears began anyway.

"Yep that's right. I got the family that you are looking for. And I will always have it like that. Good luck creating yours."

"Okay Felicia! That is enough!"

"Yeah you better act like you got some sense before I smack you in—"

"The mouth, I got it Momma." Felicia rolled her eyes.

"Girl don't play wit' me!"

"Momma, I am a grown—"

"I don't care how grown you are! I will still smack the black off you!"

Raven laughed at her grandmother. She was in the car, but her grandmother was so loud, that she could still hear her, loud and clear. "Grandma be trippin'."

"I know right," Nia laughed. "She'll put them paws on anybody. She don't care who it is."

Raven laughed again, thankful that she was finally calming down. "I don't even know why I let her piss me off like that."

"Oh girl, that chick will piss off the sun. She's just so damn messy. She didn't have to come in there, at your baby shower out of all places, and blurt out some stuff like that."

Raven shook her head and leaned back against the seat. She thought about Shannon and what he must have been thinking about her now. *Trapped him. I didn't trap him, I just wanted to have a baby, his baby, so that I could have a family. The family that I always wanted and actually deserves. I just wanted to show everybody that I could be a better mother than that thing that's in the house.* She looked at her aunt's house and rolled her eyes. "She should've just kept her mouth shut. Carla should've kept her mouth shut. They both should've just minded their business and Carla should've stayed out of my stuff. I know that's the one who told her."

"Yeah, I'm sure it was her too. She's always been jealous of you, so she'll do anything to piss you off."

"And don't come back here until you get yourself together! You're too disrespectful. A fine example you are setting for your kids!"

Raven sat up to see her mother running down the steps, Charlotte yelling behind her from the top of the porch. Nia leaned on the side of the car as Felicia angrily walked past.

"Oh, and by the way, it was Joyce who told me about your little plan. When you try to trap another dude, make sure you ain't stupid enough to leave your calendar full of secrets laying around."

"Bye Felicia! Go somewhere before I knock you out!" Nia said and Raven turned her head and looked the other way. *I hate her. I never thought it was possible to hate your own mother, but I do.*

CHAPTER 19

Raven twisted around in her bed and sighed. "Be still baby," she whispered and rubbed her stomach. The fan that sat in the window blew nothing but hot air, making it more uncomfortable. She looked over towards Nia's bed and sat up.

"Nia?"

Raven moved her feet to the side of the bed and stretched before calling out to her sister again.

"Nia?" This time a little louder.

Getting up, she steadied herself and allowed her eyes time to adjust to the dark.

"Nia?" Moving closer, she saw that Nia's bed was empty. "Where did that chick go?" Walking back to her side of the room, she picked up her phone off the floor and shook her head. *3:42* brightly stared back at her. "Where is she at three in the morning?" Sitting on her bed, she tapped her screen to call her but quickly ended it when she heard the door open. Nia walked in slowly and jumped.

"Girl! You scared me! What are you doing up?"

"I had to pee. The better question is, what are *you* doing up and where did you go?"

"It's hot as hell in here. I had to drive around and turn my air on for a while."

"Yeah right."

"I had to do something. Grandma thinks it's a crime if we turn any type of air conditioner on in here. I was going to pass out if I didn't do something."

"You should've took me with you," Raven said while standing up and stretching her arms.

"I tried to wake you up, but you didn't move. I ain't have time to be sitting around waiting for you to wobble out of the bed."

"You got jokes. Okay, I see you."

"Shit, that's what it is. I had to get up out of here."

"Yeah, I guess... ohhh, slow down baby girl."

"My niece still in there kicking like she's ready to play on Harriet High's team huh? Maybe she'll help them win a game for once. They been sorry ever since that boy was killed... what's his name again?"

"Ha, that was lame as hell, but cute. You talkin' about Kyle," Raven replied and laid slowly onto her back. The kicks that she normally felt were becoming more sharper than just normal movement.

"Yeah, they've been sorry ever since he died... I'm weak."

"What? Don't be talkin' bout my team. They may be lame but they my team," Raven giggled.

"Whateva."

Raven massaged her back and turned over on her side. "I don't think I'm supposed to...ow!"

"What? What's the matter?"

"I think I'm in labor. This is not just her kicking anymore; it's something else."

"Labor?! Again! You are too early for all that."

Yeah but I think we should call the..." The tight feeling in her back and lower stomach stopped her mid-sentence. "Ambulance," she blurted after the last of the tightness eased away. This is worse than the other night.

"No, I'll take you."

Raven slid her feet off the side of the bed again and placed them in her slippers. Grabbing her phone off the bed, she stood up, massaged her back again, and walked out into the hallway. Stopping by the stairs, she held on to the banister as another ache gripped her, causing her knees to buckle. "I need to sit down," she said as the pain moved quickly through her back and around to her belly.

"Raven?"

"I'm getting ready to go to the hospital Grandma. I think I'm in labor."

"Oh Lord."

Raven watched her grandmother sit up in bed and pick up the phone; no doubt, she was calling Charlotte.

"Can you walk?"

"Yeah, I think so." Raven stood up and allowed Nia to guide her down the stairs and into the car.

"Grandma! Call Aunt Charlotte and tell her to meet us at the hospital."

"I'm on the phone with her... she said which one?"

Nia looked at Raven and Raven closed her eyes; forgetting which hospital the free clinic was associated with. "Um, I think it's... Harmony."

"Tell her Harm—"

"No, not Harmony... Harold... Yeah, Harold Medical Center."

"You sure?"

"Yup," she sighed as another pain ripped through her. "It's Harold."

"Harold, Grandma."

"Okay, y'all call me when y'all get there."

"K," Nia answered while opening the front door and flipping the porch light on.

Why does it have to be Aunt Charlotte meeting us at the hospital? Why can't it be Shannon? Feeling a rush of emotion, Raven walked out of the house and into Nia's car, preparing herself for her daughter's very early arrival.

"Dang! We been here for twenty minutes and you are still sitting out here in the waiting room. What is wrong with this hospital and why couldn't we just go somewhere else? To a better—"

"Cause this is where my doctor sends all her patients. That's why and please sit down and be quiet."

Luckily, they were the only ones in the waiting room still waiting for a room, so Nia's rants weren't that embarrassing. Rubbing her stomach, Raven thought of her mother. *Maybe I should call her. If I tell her that I'm scared and need her help, maybe she will come and help me.* Glancing at Nia, Raven opened her mouth to ask about their mom but stopped before any words escaped. *She will just think that I'm crazy for wanting her here. If anything, she would probably tell me we need to call Shannon. I can't let Shannon know that I'm at the hospital, possibly going to have the baby early; too early. The first thing he would think is that I'm a failure and then he wouldn't want nothing else at all to do with—*

"Hey y'all, I came as fast I could. What's going on?"

"I think I'm in labor."

"Yeah, she started having pains a little while ago. We've been sitting here waiting on a room."

Charlotte looked around at the deserted check in desk. "Where is everybody?"

"Hmmm, I've been asking that question since they stuck her in a wheelchair and told us to wait on a room. I haven't seen anybody since."

236

"My goodness. Um, okay," Charlotte said as she continued to survey the waiting area. "How are you feeling now Raven?"

"I'm a little better. I keep having a hard, tight feeling across my back and—"

"Contractions," Charlotte finished her sentence. "Let me see if I can get somebody and find out something. Just hang on baby."

"Okay." Raven watched as her aunt went into action. "See... why can't ma be like that?"

"Because she's sorry and she ain't trying to come all the way down here. Especially this time of night."

Raven closed her eyes; she meant to think her question instead of asking aloud. She pretty much already knew the answer, so it was no need to ask anybody. For some reason, asking herself just calmed her a bit.

"Right... okay... thanks."

"Your room is almost finished honey and then they are coming out to get you. Did y'all try to call your momma?"

Raven put her head down. "I don't think she will want to come."

"Yeah, me neither."

"You want me to call her?"

"No!" Nia answered before Raven could even open her mouth.

Charlotte looked at Nia and shook her head. "I know you don't," she playfully popped her on the thigh, "but I'm not too sure if Raven feels the same way."

"You want me to call her?"

"It would be nice to have her here. Okay."

"What?!"

"Right on time," Raven whispered as one of the nurses walked over to her.

"Okay sweetie let's get you to a room. Are you feeling any better?"

"A little."

"Alright, let's go."

"Y'all can come on back with her."

Raven moved her feet and placed them on the footrest as the nurse began to move the wheelchair. Although she wanted her mother there, more than anyone else, it was comforting having her aunt, a registered nurse and Nia, her number one supporter there by her side.

"Okay, Raven, hop onto the bed for me. I'm going to get you hooked up to the fetal monitor."

"What's that for?" Raven asked, remembering that her nurse down at the clinic told her always ask questions when she needed to, no matter how crazy it sounded.

"It's a monitor to check your baby's heart rate."

"Oh." It looks different than the one they used the other night; it was smaller.

"Are you still feeling pain?"

Raven sat on the bed. "No, not right now."

"Okay, good. I want you to take off your clothes and put this gown on. I'll step out so you can change."

"Okay."

Raven waited for the nurse to walk out and close the door.

"You need some help?"

"No, I'm good, Auntie. I got it."

Raven quickly slipped off her shirt and put the yellow gown on.

"Do I have to take off my bra too?"

"No, you can leave that on. Let me get you a bag to put your stuff in."

Raven slipped off her shorts and her underwear and put them on the bed beside her before finding a comfortable position.

"Here you go, baby."

"Thanks, Aunt Charlotte."

Putting her belongings in the bag, she thought of Shannon. *He should be here.* She grabbed her phone and opened her contacts.

"Please don't tell me you are calling her."

Raven looked at her sister and the back at her phone. "I'm calling Shannon."

"Humph, same difference."

"Nia! That's enough. Leave your sister alone chile."

"It's his baby too and he should be here," Raven argued.

"Okay, whateva."

"Knock, knock," the nurse called in from behind the curtain.

"Do you have your gown on?"

"Yes."

"Can I get y'all anything? Anything to drink or—"

"No nothing for me, thanks," Charlotte smiled.

"I'm good," Nia answered.

"Alright."

"Okay, sweetie, lay back for me."

Raven looked at her family before laying back on the bed. A wave of anxiety rushed through her body. Taking long, slow deep breaths, she began to calm herself.

"What's the matter? Are you having pain again?"

"No, just nervous so I'm using my calming stuff to relax me," she answered slowly as she was still in her vibe.

"Aww, good job. Okay, let's get you on the monitors," the nurse smiled.

Raven pulled up her gown and watched as the nurse placed two gray straps across her belly.

"What is that?!" Nia yelled, startling Raven.

"What?"

"That? That black line going down from your navel," Nia frowned.

"It's the pregnancy line," Raven said in an irritated tone.

The nurse laughed. "The technical term for it is linea nigra. All women have it; it just gets darker during pregnancy. All those hormones."

"Yeah," Nia said and sat back down in her seat.

Raven and Charlotte both shook their heads at the look of disgust on Nia's face.

"I ain't never having no baby. Not only does your belly button poke out but you have to deal with some ugly black line too? Uh-uh, not for me."

The room grew silent while the nurse turned on the monitor. Raven smiled at the sound of her baby's heartbeat. "Aww, hi baby," she cooed as the sound echoed through the room.

"Wow, that's it?" Nia asked and stood up. "It sounds like horses galloping."

"Okay, that's it," Charlotte laughed. "Go on out in the hallway for a minute and take a break. Call Momma or something and let her know how Raven is doing. I gotta' put you to work."

The nurse looked at Charlotte and laughed.

"I'm serious. That girl is going to drive us crazy if she keeps sitting here."

"Okay, I'm going to go and get some stuff so I can start an I.V."

"I.V? Why do I need that?"

"Just in case the doctor wants to give you some meds and so we can make sure you're not dehydrated. I'm going to give you some fluids and see if that helps you feel better."

"Okay." *They didn't do all this the other night. I guess because the pains stopped as fast as they started.* Raven thought quietly and turned her head. Looking over at Charlotte, she smiled and then looked over at the monitor.

"Do you want me to call anybody, baby?"

Shannon and my mom. "No, it's late. I hope I can go home soon."

"Yeah, I hope so."

"Hi," the doctor said as he cheerfully walked in, massaged some sanitizer on his hands, and shook Charlotte's hand. "I'm Doctor Hannah. Are you mom?"

"No, I'm her aunt."

"Oh okay."

"Hi Raven, I hear that you're having some contractions. When did all this start?"

Raven began to feel a bit uneasy because a male doctor was seeing her. She was used to having female doctors. *Whoever can save my baby, I guess.* "A few hours ago," she answered.

"Okay, I'm going to take a quick look. Just to be sure that you haven't dilated any. Is that ok?"

Raven looked at her aunt. Reading her mind, Charlotte stood up.

"She's more comfortable with a female doctor. Do you have anyone that could do the pelvic exam?"

"Oh yes, absolutely. I completely understand. Let's go ahead and start the I.V, get some fluids going and I will get somebody in here from my team to take a look."

"How does that sound, Raven?"

"Good."

"Alright." The doctor patted Raven's shoulder before giving the nurse some instructions and walking out. Again, the thought of her mother and her baby's father rammed through her mind. Closing her eyes, she mentally prepared herself for a long night.

CHAPTER 20

G irl! Close that door before you let all my heat out!"

Raven rolled her eyes at the sound of her grandmother's nagging and rubbed her stomach as she thought of the false alarm she'd had a few weeks ago. Although she was ready to see her baby, she was glad that she was only in false labor as it was too early for her to be delivered.

"Yeah and sit down before you fall; wobbling around all over the place."

"Shut up," Raven laughed at her cousin Ashley. She wasn't her blood cousin, but she was her grandmother's best friend and fellow mother of the church, Ms. Ada's granddaughter. They both shared the bond of having sorry mothers, so they formed a friendship way back when they used to sit in church all day with their grandmothers.

"Does it hurt?"

"Does what...? Oh my stomach. No, only when she sticks her elbow out on my side."

"It looks like it hurts all the time."

Raven chuckled, "Nah, but it does itch a lot."

"I guess I won't ever know about that." Ashley mumbled.

Years ago, Ashley was in a bad car accident and because of it, she had to get a total hysterectomy. The accident caused major damage to her uterus, so she will never be able to have children.

"Well, you know you can see Miracle whenever you want. She will be both of ours." Raven hoped to brighten the mood, as she knew how hard it was for Ashley unable ever to have kids.

"That's right, she is my goddaughter and I am going to spoil her!"

"I know you will," Raven laughed. "So, what's it like in the old boring suburbs these days?"

"Boring is right. It's the same ole thing over there. A bunch of lames walking around trying to be something they not. Oh, girl and don't let me get started on the ones who call themselves being in a gang."

"Shut up! Townsend got gangs now?"

"I said call themselves doing that. They ain't about that life over there. If somebody brought them over here and left them, they would pee all over themselves."

Raven laughed and grabbed the bag of gifts that Ashley and her grandmother brought for Miracle. She opened the bag and smiled. "Aww, this is too cute!" She pulled out a purple short set with matching booties and a hat to go with it. "Thank you, I love it."

"You're welcome. As soon as I saw it, I knew I had to get it."

"It is so cute." Raven grabbed one of the baby hangers that she gotten from the baby shower and hung it up in her closet.

"It looks like you are all ready for her."

"Yep, my due date is next week so she can come at any time now."

Raven looked out the window at a few kids walking by, all excited about trick or treating.

"Are you scared?"

She kept her eyes on the crowd outside. "A little," she admitted for the first time. Really, she was just beginning to come to terms with the fact that she was getting ready to go through what so many other women had already gone through, giving birth. She thought about how hard it might be. No, she didn't know firsthand, but she heard so many people talking about it and their stories alone had her petrified.

"You know my cousin on my father side had a baby and she said it hurt like hell."

Raven turned away from the window and frowned at Ashley. "Gee, thanks for that," she said sarcastically and threw one of Nia's pillows at her.

"What?! You may as well know the truth before you go in there. I also heard about this one girl who died during—"

"Ohh-kayy, that's enough. I do not need to hear about somebody dying while having a baby. I'm getting ready to have one, remember?!"

"My bad," Ashley laughed. "I was just sayin'."

"Yeah, well, don't," Raven said and chuckled.

"You know what we should do?"

"What?" Raven walked over to her closet and ran her hand through all the baby clothes.

"We should go trick or treating!"

"What? Chick, are you crazy?! Imagine me walking out there with this stomach around a bunch of kids knocking on people's doors and asking for candy. Girl bye!"

"Come on, we don't have to actually go trick or treating. We can just walk around for a while. Just something to do. Ain't no telling when Grandma and Aunt Shirley will be back from church. They just left so they ain't even at the church yet."

Raven shook her head and grabbed her sneakers. "A'ight, nothing wrong with walking around for a while but if you knock on anybody's door or mess with any of the little kids, I'ma smack you."

"I told you that I ain't going to do that. Just wobble yourself down the stairs and let's go before they get back."

Walking down the stairs, Raven grabbed her coat from the coat rack and followed Ashley out onto the front porch. The cold air smacked Raven in the face causing her to gasp but it was so much more refreshing than the air in the house. Her grandmother didn't like too much heat in the winter and too much air in the summer. No matter who was uncomfortable, she kept her house how she wanted it.

"Trick or treat!" A group of kids yelled at the house next door.

"We should've got some candy." Ashley mumbled.

"Why, so we can eat it all before any of these kids get it?"

"Exactly!"

Raven laughed and nudged Ashley on the shoulder. "You be trippin' but you are right. We could've gotten at least one bag and gave away half and kept the other half for us."

"Girl please, we would've had all that candy!"

"Yeah, you right."

The girls continued to walk through the neighborhood, admiring all the costumes and houses decorated with all sorts of stuff from vampires to fake blood and graves to the lighter stuff like freshly carved pumpkins and haystacks.

"I'm surprised they decorate like this out here. They do as much decorating as we do in Townsend."

"Yeah, I am shocked too. They do a lot of this type of stuff where Aunt Joyce live at, but I didn't know they do all this over here until I moved over here."

"Is that a haunted house?!" Ashley called out.

"Where?"

"Over there, look across the street by the gas station. I think that's a haunted house. Come on, let's go in."

"Girl, I'm not going in there." Raven laughed.

"Why not?! It looks like it's lit up in there."

"Yeah, it does look like it's fun, but I'm not going up in there and then somebody mess around and hit me in the stomach cause they not watching where they going. But you go ahead. I'll stand out here and wait for you."

"Uh-uh, I'm not leaving you out here just so I can go into a house that somebody decided to make into a haunted house for one night. Now, if it was a real one, like the one over there by the graveyard... You trying to go?"

"No! I'm definitely not going over there!" Raven laughed and shook her head. "Nope! I would probably go into labor if I go over there with you. Even if I wait outside, they probably have stuff sitting around out in the yard, ready to jump out all crazy."

"Yeah, they do," Ashley giggled.

The girls laughed and continued to walk slowly. Looking around at more decorations, Raven thought about her favorite time of year, Christmas. "I wonder why they don't decorate like this during Christmas time."

"Maybe they don't feel like messing with all the lights and stuff. You know it's so much easier to throw some stuff on the porch and in the yard than it is to stand on a ladder and put some lights up. And don't let me get started on putting up a tree. Can't stand doing that!"

"I love decorating the..." A popping feeling popped within Raven's stomach followed by a warm trickle that slowly eased down her legs, stopped her in her tracks.

"What's wrong?"

Raven looked at Ashley with panic filled eyes and then looked down on the ground. "I think my water just broke."

"What?!"

"Ohh, it's cold."

"Um, okay, um... let's go back home so we can—"

"Uh-uh, I'm not going to make it home. Call Nia or the ambu... Ow!"

"Hey... Miss... Excuse me...Really?! Did she just walk right past me like that?!"

"Forget them," Raven huffed through the cramping pain that was beginning to get stronger by the minute. "Just call the ambulance and Nia." She held onto her stomach and began to do her breathing exercises that she had practiced so many times before, but it wasn't working as well as she thought it would. "And Aunt Charlotte, call her too." Raven leaned against an old gas station's wall and closed her eyes, the water continued to flow, causing her to shiver.

"K."

"Uh, my cousin is having a baby...she's in labor...no...wait...

Contractions? Are you having contractions?"

"Just some cramping."

"She said just some cramping... ok and she...oh and her water broke! Um, I can't see any signs... What street is—?"

"Marble. Tell them we are standing by the old Pick and Go gas station."

"Marble Street..."

"Ok... thanks."

"They are on the way. Are you ok?"

"No, but I will be once I get to the hospital." Raven continued to lean on the gas station's wall. Scared, nervous and happy all at the same time.

"Did they say how long it will be before she comes out?" Nia asked while lightly rubbing her hands through the hospital's curtains.

"I'm not really dilated yet, so I don't know."

"Well, I'm just so glad Ashley was with you when this all started. I was hoping that you wouldn't be by yourself when you went into labor."

"Yeah, me too Aunt Charlotte. I was hoping that she would stay, but I think it's too much for her. With her—"

"Right, that's right. Well, I'm sure she will be here once Miracle gets here. I know she wants to see her."

"Yep..." Raven stopped and took slow deep breaths as a small contraction began to take root in the bottom of her belly.

"That's it; breathe through it," Charlotte stood up and grabbed Raven's hand. "Slow, deep, steady breaths."

Raven opened her eyes to see a look of pure fear on Nia's face. "I promise you, I'm fine," she chuckled and threw a small box of tissues at Nia.

"You better be."

Raven and Charlotte both laughed at Nia while she flopped down in the big recliner that sat next to the window.

"Momma told me to tell you that she's praying for you."

"Okay, tell her I said thanks."

Closing her eyes, Raven thought of the people that should be there with her and Miracle. It was cool having her aunt and her sister there with her for support, but it would've really been nice to have Shannon sitting beside her, helping her breathe through contractions and getting all excited like a new father-to-be should. *Maybe he will come.* She looked at Nia, but her mouth wouldn't open to give her thoughts a voice. *She is not going to call him and even if she did, he most likely won't come due to my mother's big mouth.* Raven braced herself as another contraction began to ripple through. She breathed and waited for it to end before she continued her thoughts. *My mother. Humph, why can't she just be a real mother and do what real mothers do?* She envisioned her mother holding Miracle and doting all over her. *I kind of wish she was here.* She looked at her Aunt Charlotte and quickly removed the question of if she would call her and let her know that she was in labor. *No doubt, that Aunt Charlotte is still mad and don't want nothing to do with her right now. Mommy's girl,* she whispered internally. *It would be nice to be a mommy's girl. Just like Trinity. Why couldn't I be the one she calls her baby and her mommy's girl?* Sighing, she moved her thoughts away from her mother and Shannon because if she didn't, the tears that were forming would fall and get everybody all upset. *This is a time to celebrate and bring my baby, who would be a mommy's girl, into this world. She is the answer to fix all my mommy and baby daddy issues.*

"Raven, do you need anything? The nurse said you can have ice chips to keep your mouth from getting dry. Do you want me to get you some?"

"Nah, I'm good."

"Okay, well, I'm going to go down to the cafeteria and see if I can get me some coffee."

"Come on Nia, you want to walk with me?"

"Yeah, I can. Do you think they are still open? It's almost twelve."

"Yup, they stay open all night now. They *would* change the schedule once I'm no longer here," Charlotte laughed. "It's been plenty of nights working here that I needed some coffee and they would always be closed anytime I needed it."

Everybody chuckled and Charlotte grabbed her purse.

"Okay baby, we'll be right back. You push your call bell if you need anything."

"K."

"Don't be having her until we get back."

"Shut up!" Raven laughed at Nia.

Nia smiled at Raven before following Charlotte out of the room.

Raven glanced at all the equipment that surrounded her. She paid attention to the monitor on the wall, but special attention to the one directly beside her. The sound of her baby's heartbeat was coming from that one as well as paper, which showed the nurses her contractions. Smiling, she rubbed her stomach. "I can't wait to finally see you," she whispered. Looking at her phone, she thought of Shannon. *Maybe I should just text him. Maybe he'll come and want to be here to see Miracle born.* She then looked at her call bell. *I don't think I'm supposed to get up so I guess I will have to call one of the nurses to give me my phone. Who put it all the way over there anyways?*

"Knock! Knock!"

"Yes?"

"Hey, how are you feeling?"

"Ok, I guess."

"I see that you had a few contractions since the last time I came in here."

"Oh yeah, a few."

"Good; the stronger your contractions, the closer we are to having a baby."

Raven smiled at her nurse and repositioned herself in the bed.

"Alright. Call out if you need anything."

"Ok, thanks," Raven replied shyly and waited for her nurse to walk out before she tried to pull the table over and get her phone. *Why didn't I just ask her to pull the table over for me?* "Duh moment; I'm weak," she laughed and sat back in bed.

"Yeah, she's right in there. Yep, right there."

Raven looked towards the door and waited for someone to come in, hoping that the nurse was talking to a guest there to visit her. *Maybe it's Ashley.* Readjusting her pillow, she kept her eyes on the door, but the door remained closed. *Well... I guess it was for somebody next...* Raven stopped mid thought as her door slowly opened.

"Yo."

Gasping, she did everything in her power not to get all giddy, but her efforts failed at the sound of Shannon's voice.

"Yes," she said as nonchalantly as she could but even her voice wouldn't behave.

"Hey."

Raven almost fell out of the bed when Shannon finally entered the room.

"Hi."

"How you doing?"

"I haven't had any more contractions in a minute, so I'm ok."

There was a crazy, awkward pause between Raven and Shannon. Raven tried to look anywhere in the room but directly at Shannon. She couldn't keep her eyes off him, no matter how hard she tried. *That black hair gets me every time.*

"Uh, you can sit down if you want to."

"Nah, I'm good."

Another pause filled the space before either of them said a word.

"So, I guess that's her heartbeat," Shannon nodded his head towards the fetal monitor.

"Yep, that's it. Strong huh?"

"Yeah, she tough, like her daddy."

Raven giggled and began to feel an overwhelmingly sense of relief and happiness. "Yep, just like her daddy."

"Hey, I'm sorry about what happened at the baby—"

"Oh nah," Shannon stopped Raven before she could finish her sentence. "It's all good. She's here now; well, on her way. It doesn't matter how she got here."

Raven smiled but it was quickly replaced by slow deep breathing. She gripped her stomach and braced herself for the pain of another contraction.

"You alright?"

"Contraction," Raven whispered.

"You want me to get the—"

Raven put her finger up while the contraction reached its peak and slowly began to come down. "Whew, that was a hard one."

Shannon pulled a chair from the corner of the room and sat it next to Raven. Raven giggled and nodded her head towards the chair. "Are you going to sit down or...?"

"Yeah, I'm just—"

"I'm not going to bite you or anything. You can sit down."

"I guess I'm just nervous. Seeing you go through that contraction, that was crazy."

"If you think seeing it is crazy, try actually going through it."

"Yeah."

"I can't believe they didn't have not one drop of coffee made. Took them almost an hour just to make the stuff! They know people are here all night and need coffee."

"No, not everybody drinks that mess Aunt Charlotte."

"Well, I do. They going to mess around and... well, hello."

Raven shyly smiled as Nia and Charlotte entered the room.

"How you doing?" Shannon said as he nervously readjusted himself in the seat.

"I'm blessed. How are you doing young man?"

"I'm doing good."

"Glad you could make it," Nia joined in and flopped down in the recliner.

"Yeah, thanks for hittin' me up."

"Wait," Raven smiled. "You called him?"

"He is supposed to be here. We can't have Miracle coming all up in the world without both her parents around her."

Raven nodded and Shannon smiled.

"Momma called. She just wanted to check on you."

"Oh okay. Tell Grandma thanks for checking on me."

"Alright. I'm going to go over there after I leave here. Just to check on her. Nia, you going home tonight?"

"No, I'm going to stay here until that chick drops the baby."

Raven and Shannon both laughed.

"You are a mess," Charlotte shook her head and sipped some of her coffee.

"Knock. Knock. Hey, Raven. Wanted to come and check to see if we've had any progress." The nurse walked in and smiled.

"Are you dad?"

"Uh, yeah."

"Okay, you can stay in here if you want. We just want to—"

"Oh nah, I will step out for a minute."

"It's okay, you can stay in here," Raven said, hoping that she would be able to convince him to stay in there with her.

"Yeah, you should stay. Hold her hand or something!" Nia said loudly.

Raven side eyed Nia and Nia stood up. "I'll be standing by the door."

"Well, I'm going to head over and check in on Momma, but I'll be back in a little while."

"Thanks Aunt Charlotte." Raven leaned over, gave her aunt a quick hug, and proceeded to ready herself for her exam. The family walked out while Shannon stayed.

"Thank you for staying."

"Do you need me to hold your hand?"

Raven smiled and nodded. "That would be nice."

Shannon smiled back and grabbed onto Raven's hand. *My family is finally happening*, she whispered within as the nurse prepped to check on the baby.

The time is finally here, Raven thought quietly to herself while glancing around at the machinery that surrounded her. Hours had passed since her nurse checked on her. "A slow birth," she said when she checked the last time. Miracle was still nowhere near ready to come out. Shannon had fallen asleep, leaving Raven's mind to launch into the fairy tale land of what it would be like for her and Shannon to be together again. This time, with a baby, sealing the deal for a full family. Looking over at him, she gave him a quick smile and then turned towards one of the floor's nurse assistants, Leandra, who had walked in a few minutes before.

"These are for you!" She squealed while placing a small bouquet of yellow and white flowers on the counter.

"Thanks," Raven said and sat up a little further in bed. "Who are they from?"

"Uh, looks like they are from the staff at Harriet High."

"Oh, okay." Disappointed, Raven had hoped that the gift was from her mother or any member of her family for that matter.

"They don't care at all," she quipped and rubbed her stomach. "Well, at least we have Nia, grandma, and Aunt Charlotte. And you know what else baby, we have your daddy." Gently rubbing her belly, she smiled and looked back at her flowers. "And my school," she chuckled.

"Nice flowers and it was nice of your school to send them to you."

"Yeah."

The assistant moved around a little more before she looked over at Raven. "Well, you know to call me if you need anything. Do you have your call bell?"

Raven uncomfortably looked around for the device that had become one of her best friends, the good ole call bell, and held it up. "Got it." She smiled. All she had to do was push the button and she got whatever she needed or wanted. Not only her, but Shannon too. *So much better than what I get at home*, she said when she was first introduced to it and began to get comfortable with the idea; the idea of people tending to her for once. *Finally, some attention*, she thought quietly to herself when she'd first gotten there, and the nurses were checking her in and hooking her up to all the machines.

"Okay, cool. Push it if you need anything. Do you want some ice chips? Is your mouth dry?"

"Nah," Raven replied but stopped as a small contraction was building up within her wound. "I'm good," she managed to get out before the contraction moved to its worse stage.

"Okay, what about your boyfriend? Should I get him a blanket?"

Raven looked over at Shannon and shook her head. "No, I think he's good."

"Okay," Leandra smiled and walked out of the room, gently closing the door behind her.

Raven looked around and sighed. "Almost here baby girl," she whispered soothingly and looked down at her belly. "Ow," she winced out in pain as another harsh contraction took over her body, causing her almost to come out of the bed. Strips of paper flowed from the fetal monitor, giving the nurse an indication that she'd had another contraction.

"Hey Raven. Coming in."

"Hey," Raven mumbled through the pain.

"That was a big one, huh?" Her nurse Loretta spoke softly while looking at the last few strips of paper that had flowed from the monitor. Raven bonded closely with Loretta over the past few hours, well in the last day and half, as her labor began that long ago. Raven looked at Loretta as a gentle mother figure being that her own mother, Felicia was rarely around to give love and comfort to her pregnant sixteen-year-old daughter.

"Yes, it hurt pretty bad," Raven replied. Closing her eyes, she inhaled deeply and exhaled slowly as the contraction slowly came to an end just as Loretta had instructed her to do when they'd first met.

"All the pain is worth it baby," she mumbled while gently rubbing her stomach. "In just a few hours, I will have the one thing that would make me whole."

"Yeah, it won't be long now before we get your little bundle of joy born and out into the world," Loretta smiled and gently rubbed Raven's shoulder. "Hang in there baby. You are doing great and I'm so proud of you Raven."

Raven smiled at her nurse, but the smile was quickly replaced with a frown as another contraction took over her belly and this time, her lower back was in the mix. "Oh no," she whimpered and grabbed onto the side of her hospital bed.

"Breathe," Loretta said. "Just breathe through it."

Again, Raven inhaled deeply and began to exhale but let out a growl instead. "Oh! It's hurting too bad! Way worse than the other times."

"Okay, let me get Dr. Bass in here."

"Janice! Call Dr. Bass stat!"

"Ow, oh, ow!" Raven yelled out in pain.

"Hang on, Raven. Dr. Bass is on the way."

Pain hit Raven from all different sides of her body and at different intensities.

"Stat! Get her in here, stat!" Those were the last words Raven heard before everything around her changed from a heavy chaos to compete darkness.

CHAPTER 20

Slowly opening her eyes, Raven felt like she had swallowed a full basket of cactuses. She tried to move but her body felt like it was being held down by a mountain of bricks.

"Hi Raven, how are you feeling?"

Raven struggled to move her head towards the person who had spoken to her.

"It..." she stopped as the pain from her neck caught her off guard. Although her neck pain was bad, it was nowhere near as harsh as the pain that was coming from her stomach.

"It's okay, don't try to talk. My name is Angela and I'm your nurse here in recovery."

Recovery? What am I doing here? Even though her body wasn't cooperating with her, her mind was in full force. Moving her arms with all her might, she touched her stomach. "Where...?" she started but again, the pain took over and stopped her.

"Don't try to talk," Angela said while standing directly in front of Raven.

Raven was glad to finally see the soft-spoken woman who'd been talking to her since she'd awakened. Her voice relaxed Raven, but she still was very confused and needed somebody to tell her what was going on.

"I have something for you."

Angela laid a picture in front of Raven. "Congratulations. She is beautiful."

Raven stared at the picture; looking at a very tiny version of Shannon with eyes shaped like her eyes. Smiling, she looked at the nurse and as if she was reading Raven's mind, she smiled back. "She is perfect, and you will get to see her and hold her and love on her very soon."

Suddenly, the pain didn't seem to hurt all that much. It was all replaced by the excitement and the joy of seeing Miracle. *Finally*, she thought quietly as she kept the smile on her face. *You're finally here, with the black hair and all.*

"How are you feeling?"

"Cold," Raven answered while continuing to admire the picture of her newborn baby.

"I'll get you some warm blankets from the warmer."

"Thanks."

"Hmm-hmm."

Raven couldn't take her eyes off the picture. "It's like having Christmas all over again," she mumbled. "Except this time, I get to have a gift so precious and so much better than any gift I've ever gotten before. Mommy's girl," she whispered.

"Okay Raven, are you ready to hold your baby?"

"Hold her?"

"Yep, you finally get to hold her."

A huge ball of emotion took Raven by shock and surprise. The same feeling she'd gotten on the day she found out that she was going to be a mother. "Okay, yes, I want to hold her."

"Alright, let's go. She's in the NICU, but the nurses and the doctors there has gotten her—"

"NICU?"

"Yes, the neonatal intensive care—"

"Intensive care? Why is she in there?"

"Well, she had a few issues breathing on her own so the doctors thought it would be best to have her hang out there for a while. I saw her and she's doing great. Such a beautiful baby."

Raven's nerves were on ten and that was putting it lightly. She began to take small deep breaths but when she went to inhale, she felt the pressure and pain in the bottom of her stomach. Her throat was finally beginning to feel better, allowing her to talk more freely.

"Why does my stomach hurt so bad?"

"Aww, I'm sure you are having some pain there. You had an emergency C-section, hun. Your baby's heart rate dropped, and you too were in distress, so it was —"

"I fainted."

"Yes, that's right. But the doctors will talk with you more and answer all of your questions. Let's go and see that beautiful baby of yours."

"Okay, do I need to get in a wheelchair or something?"

"No, not right now. We are going to wheel you down there right here in your bed."

"Oh, okay."

Raven slightly put her hand on her stomach and winced. Working to ignore the pain, she looked at her picture of her baby and focused on it while the nurse prepared her and her belongings to go down and see her baby. The moment she's been waiting for since forever.

"Miracle," Raven muttered as she was wheeled into her room. Flowers and balloons awaited her as her nurse pushed her in from the surgery area.

"Hi sweetheart. How are you feeling?"

Raven tried to answer her aunt, but her voice was replaced by a small whimper before tears began to fall from her eyes.

"Oh baby. What is it? What's bothering you?"

Looking around the room through tear-stained eyes, she searched for Shannon.

"Where is Shannon?"

"He's coming back, He went to go and get his mom so she can see the baby."

Raven watched as her nurse scribbled something down on a piece of paper. Turning her attention back to her aunt, she frowned.

"What about—?"

"Nia went to go and check on Momma. She's on her way back. You know, you had a very hard night last night. You must be pretty tired."

"Yes, a little."

"Alright, hit your call bell if you need anything," her nurse said gently before walking over to the door.

"Um, when can I go back and see my baby?" She asked right before her voice cracked again and the sobbing continued.

"Very soon. I will get the NICU doctor up here to talk with you. Now, you be sure to ask as many questions as you want. As many questions as you need to ask."

Raven nodded her head.

"Thank you so much."

"You're welcome," the nurse said to Charlotte before walking out.

"That baby is one beautiful little girl. She looks so much like her daddy and she got a little of Felicia in her too."

Felicia... I wonder if anybody has called her to tell her that she has a new granddaughter. Would she even care? "Does my mom know that Miracle is here?"

Charlotte walked over to Raven and removed her pillow fluffed it and put it back behind her head. "I called and told her but—"

"But... but what?"

"She said not to call her no more with that mess. She has better things to do."

Raven slowly shook her head and grabbed her picture of Miracle.

"Oh chile, you know how your momma is. She is in her own little world dealing with her own little issues. You stop worrying so much about her. You and your baby got plenty of love and if she doesn't want nothing to do with her, then let her go. You just be a better mom to your baby."

"Easier said than done." *I mean, why can't she just be a mom. Everybody else mom is there for them. Why me? Why do I have to be given a mom like that?*

"I'm telling you baby. Women like her is not going to change their ways until they want to. It's nothing you, me, or anybody can do about it so no need to keep it on your mind. We got to let go and let God. The rest will fall into place."

"Hey girl!"

Startled, Raven looked towards the door to see Nia walking in. "Where did you get that?" Raven laughed, finally beginning to feel her spirits lift.

"Oh this? They sell these down at the gift shop."

"World's Best Aunt," Raven read aloud. "It's so cute!"

"Yeah it better be. For twenty dollars, you better think it's lit. Did you see Miracle yet?"

Raven smiled. "Yep, the nurse took me down there."

"Good." Nia sat down in the recliner and put her feet up. "I am tired! I am so glad you finally had her. I was about to strangle you if you didn't hurry up and drop her."

"Shut up!" Raven laughed. "I'm happy she's finally here too."

"Grandma said she looks like her mom when her mom was little."

"Yeah, I can see that too," Charlotte laughed.

"I think she looks just like Shannon. Got all that pretty black hair and everything. I can't wait to see what color eyes she has."

Raven smiled at Nia. "I know right. They have my shape, maybe they will be my color too."

"Yeah, they will probably be a mix. Blue like yours but a little darker because of Shannon's. The rest of the family has regular color eyes," Nia chuckled. "You the only one with those exotic looking eyes. I guess you get them from your daddy side."

Yeah, whoever that is. "I guess."

"Hello…"

Everyone looked at the door as it was opening. Raven almost leapt out of the bed when she saw what, or rather, who her favorite nurse, Loretta was holding gently in her arms. The mop of black hair was covered with a pink hat and her tiny body was covered with a blanket. "Look who I have," Loretta smiled.

Charlotte and Nia both moved over to Raven's side.

"Look at her," Charlotte cooed. "She is so adorable; just so precious."

Nia smiled but remained quiet.

"Are you ready to finally hold your baby? I heard you were anxious to hold her earlier, but she was having some testing done."

"Yea," Raven said as she looked around for help. She knew nothing about babies; not even how to hold them. "She's so tiny; I'm scared I'm going to—"

"No, no, I promise, she's not going to break." Loretta said while slowly placing her in Raven's arms. In an instant, all nervousness and fear was gone. The feeling to love, guide, and protect was in the fear's place, allowing her to relax and enjoy the moment. "Hi," she said softly to her sleeping baby. "You are so pretty."

Nia moved her hat off her head, just enough to expose her black hair. "She is beautiful, Raven."

Raven looked at her sister and then back at her baby. "Miracle, you will forever be... mommy's girl."

SEVEN MONTHS LATER

"Miracle! No! Put that down!" Raven sighed loudly as she pulled her grandmother's soda bottle out of her daughter's hand. "Why do you have to touch everything? All the time," she giggled. Picking her up, she smoothed her small ponytail down and sat her down on the couch. Miracle babbled loudly and wildly patted one of her Christmas toys, a lights and sounds educational gift. *Thanks Aunt Charlotte. Just had to get her one of the loudest toys around.* Raven shook her head and looked down at her phone. "Daddy will be here soon Miracle." The baby continued to babble and laugh. "Mommy's little girl," she smiled while grabbing Miracle's bag and putting a stack of diapers into it, followed by some extra clothes. It was Shannon's weekend to have the baby and Raven couldn't be happier. In the last week, she's had to deal with Miracle being sick with a cold; causing her asthma problem to go haywire. When that happened, it's an all-night, all day job of keeping Miracle breathing intact or it'll be another trip to the children's hospital. Raven grabbed Miracle's hairbrush and threw it in her bag. Next, she grabbed all her asthma medicines and put them in the special hand-made bag, compliments of Shannon's mother. Raven smiled at the white bag with pink letters that spelled out *Miracle's Meds* on it. "Miracle, here's your bag from Grandma." Raven looked at her baby and her baby looked at her and then back at her toy, banging it again with all her strength.

"Little Bit! Hey auntie's Little Bit!" Nia called out and Miracle waved her hands up and down wildly and squealed at the sound of her aunt's voice. Nia picked her niece up and gave her small quick kisses all over her face. Miracle laughed and babbled the entire time, loving all the attention from her aunt.

"You working this weekend?"

Raven put the last of Miracle's medicines in the bag and shook her head. "Nope, not this weekend. I do have to study through so I'm glad this is one of Shannon's weekends to spend with Miracle."

"Yeah," Nia said and put Miracle back on the chair, flopping down beside her. "Girl, you need to go out and have some fun! You've been doing nothing but studying and being a mother. Go out and do something."

"Humph, I can't do nothing but study and take care of my baby. I don't have time for nothing else. You know I got to pass summer school. I ain't tryin' to stay up in Harriet any longer than I have to."

"Why can't you just take the extra classes throughout the school year next year? I know a lot of twelfth graders that have done that."

"Yeah but If I don't take the classes now, I won't be in the twelfth grade when school starts back," Raven laughed.

"Well at least Shannon and his momma are acting like they got some sense."

"Yep, at least she got one of her grandmother's doing right by her."

"Girl, your mother is selfish and will always be that way."

"*Our* mother."

"Girl bye! *Your* mother," Nia said and rolled her eyes. "I ain't got nothing for that chick. I can't believe she's only seen Miracle one time since she's been born, and she is seven months! Almost a year old and she don't even know her own grandmother. That's *your* momma."

Raven sat down on the floor and looked through the baby's bags. "Girl, I guess. It is what it is. Let her stay over there with her baby daddy and his kids." Shaking her head, she focused her attention back on Miracle's belongings. Making sure everything was in there that would be needed while she was with her dad, her grandmother, and Shannon's new girlfriend. Yes, Shannon had a new girlfriend and it was driving Raven absolutely crazy. Shannon announced he and his girl would take good care of Miracle, catching Raven off guard. *He didn't even let my stiches heal from the c-section first before he announced that news; in front of everybody*, she said while the tears were falling down her face after she'd first was told the news. She was over the shock now and able to cope better but the fact that he's moved on, not giving her a second thought still stung Raven's heart, but she managed. *A baby don't keep a man who don't want to be kept*, she heard her grandmother's voice. *Yep, learned that the hard way.* Yeah, her and Shannon were cool, but she wanted more; she felt like she deserved more.

I had a whole baby with him, and he goes and gets with somebody else. Somebody who has never had any kids. Humph, I guess because she is in the Army Reserves too. Makes it so much easier for his mother to like her. That girl has a good head on her shoulders, Shannon's mother said to her countless times. *Like I am a nobody. Well, I guess in her eyes, I'm not.*

"Y'all need to put that girl down and let her walk."

Miracle again got excited, at the sound of her great grandmother's voice.

"Ain't that right baby? You ready to walk ain't you? Come on and walk to Grandma. Put her down, Nia." Nia picked Miracle up and put her on the floor, holding her hands while she worked to get her balance.

"Come on, baby."

Miracle squealed and moved her feet slowly.

"That's it, come on."

The doctor said it might take her a little longer to be able to walk and all because of developmental delays.

"Oh, what do they know?! I've been taking care of kids longer than that ole doctor has been alive. That baby can walk; just have to help her."

"Um, she is a doctor, a pediatrician. She should know about those types of things," Nia mumbled.

"Don't make me smack you chile."

Nia and Raven both laughed.

"Ain't nothing wrong with that baby. Watch what I tell y'all. She'll be walking before you know it."

"Come on baby. Move those legs."

Raven smiled as Miracle moved her legs forward and then sat down on the floor. Nia picked her up and kissed her all over again, causing her to laugh.

"What time is Shannon coming?"

"He said he would be here after he gets off work."

"I hope he don't bring that hoe with him this time. I can't stand her."

"Watch yo' mouth Nia before I smack you in it."

Nia shook her head and sat down next to Miracle. "That boy is outside."

Raven and Nia both looked towards the window.

"Yep, that's him... and he got that—"

"What did I tell you?!"

Nia ignored her grandmother, rolled her eyes again and walked over to the door, hastily opening it and walked away.

"Daddy's here, Miracle. Come on. Let's get this over with." Raven grabbed Miracle's bags and picked her up before heading to the door. Shannon got out of the car, leaned back in and came back out, smiling. Raven rolled her eyes and looked at Miracle, working to keep all her attention on her.

"Wassup tank-tank. Wassup."

Miracle's mouth opened wide and she let out a joyful scream that startled Raven.

"Yeah, daddy's baby right there. Was sup," Shannon said as he grabbed Miracle and kissed her on the forehead. "Hey baby."

"Wassup Raven."

"Hey."

Raven looked at Shannon's truck and frowned at his girlfriend. She didn't know her name and she didn't want to know. All she wanted was for Shannon to dump her and to be with her and their baby. Give her the happy family that she's always wanted. Raven hated the fact that Shannon was with someone else, leaving her to be another statistic, a teenage mother who is not with the baby's father. *At least he does take care of Miracle and is a part of her life. I guess I can be happy about that. I'm glad my baby won't be just another statistic. She has her daddy in her life.* Raven smiled at Miracle and Shannon.

"Alright, so I will bring her back by seven on Sunday. Is that a good time for you?"

"Uh, yeah, that's good."

"Okay, my mom told me to make sure you have a dress in the bag for church. She's taking her to church Sunday."

"Yep, it's in there and ready to go; the yellow one that she bought her."

"Alright cool."

Raven kissed Miracle. "See you on Sunday my little mommy's girl."

Miracle spoke in only the language she understood as Shannon walked away with her, smiling and laughing while walking to his truck. "Ugh," Raven sighed when the girl got out of the passenger seat, waved at her and smiled at Miracle.

"Hi pretty blue eyes," she cooed.

Why is she even talking to my baby?

"You have the prettiest blue eyes I have ever seen."

"Oh yeah, maybe you should take a look at mine. She gets those eyes from me; her real mother." Raven folded her arms and lightly shook her head at the sight of another girl playing and talking to her baby. *Well, she's his girlfriend so nothing I can do about it. He has just as much rights to her as I do.*

Raven continued to stand on the porch and watch as Shannon secured the baby into her car seat that Shannon had designed to match the seats in his truck.

"Yeah, maybe your little sister or brother will have those pretty blue eyes too. Just like his or her big sister." Raven gasped and looked at Shannon. Shannon gave a quick nod before he got in his truck and drove away with their daughter, his girlfriend and apparently, a new baby that was on the way.

Yolanda's Note

Hello Beauties!

Growing up, the one thing that I've learned was that most girls, if not all, want to feel as if they belong to someone. Unfortunately, not everyone has the pleasure of having such.

Raven grew up without the love of her mom and because of it, she decided to plan to have a baby in hopes that she would create the feeling of belonging to someone; her baby and her baby's father. It all seemed good when she was planning, but she quickly realized that a baby didn't change situations from her past and it didn't keep Shannon around either. You see, everyone has something from their past that they would like to change. There is nothing that can be done about it except live the very best life you can right now. Take away the positive from the past and apply it to your future.

Love,

Yolanda

Meet the Author

Yolanda Randolph is the creator of the #Her Intuition Movement, a movement dedicated to empowering and motivating women to be at their best and to remind them of their worth. Yolanda is also a Credentialed Medical Coder, mother of three teenagers and the owner of Madisyn, her beloved Yorkshire terrier.

Yolanda is an avid reader and loves to write as well. She is dedicated to helping young women reach their highest potential through telling her stories. A survivor of domestic violence and many trials throughout her life, she has become persistent with encouraging others; in hopes that she is an inspiration.

Originally, from Baltimore, Maryland, Yolanda now lives in Greenville, NC with her family.

Stay connected with Yolanda via Social Media:

- *Facebook - Yolanda Randolph Publications*
- *Instagram - YolandaRandolphPublications*
- *Twitter – YolandaRWrites*
- *Website – www.yolandarandolph.com*

Twila's Dilemma

Field of Lies;
Touchdown in Truth

Yolanda Randolph

The Harriet High Series

Prologue

"Stop! Hey! Adriana, Stop! You're going to get us kill—"

"Shut up Twila! Just sit back and chill! I got you!"

Twila held onto the passenger seat in her best friend's car. Catching quick glimpses out of the window, she saw nothing but hard rain falling and blustery trees whipping by extremely fast in the dusk filled sky. The sidewalks were unusually bare, and the streets were just as empty. "Ugh!" Twila yelled as Adriana rounded a sharp corner without slowing down.

"Adriana!"

"Twila! Calm down girl! Just chill and enjoy the ride."

Twila's mind was full of fear and anger, a feeling that she's never felt before. *I am going to punch her dead in the mouth when I get out of here; if I'm alive.* Closing her eyes, she thought of her mother and her father; thinking of all the trouble she was going to be in once they found out that she decided to get in the car with Adriana, knowing that she had been drinking. *Why did I get in this car? Why did I...* "Woah!" She screamed as Adriana rolled over a row of jagged train tracks, not bothering at all to look out for her tires. Closing her eyes tighter, Twila thought of her grandmother and the words she would speak if she was in a bad situation. *God can help you through all things. Always trust in Him*, she heard her grandmother's voice. Closing her eyes even tighter, to the point where she thought they would burst, she began to call out in prayer. *God, please help me*, she chanted quietly while holding on for dear life to the side of her seat. She looked over at Adriana and was in shock at the sight of a big grin plastered on her face. "This chick is crazy!" She yelled, not caring what Adriana thought of her statement. In an instant, Adriana slammed on her brakes. The car slid onto the sidewalk and jolted out of its movement. A thick cloud of smoke replaced the rain that had fallen minutes prior and entered high into the sky, causing a crowd to rapidly form. Twila opened her eyes and immediately felt all over her body. "Thank God!" She called out as everything felt like it was in place.

"Hey! Are you alright?!" A man yelled from the crowd.

"Somebody call the police and the ambulance!" Another man shouted.

Feeling a trickle fall down the side of her head, Twila gasped and rubbed the spot, noticing a gash there. "Aw man," she sighed. "Adr... Adriana!" Suddenly, she remembered that Adriana was the one driving; the one who caused the crash. "Oh no! Adriana!" She looked over at her friend and screamed out in horror at the sight of her limp body.

"Adriana!"

"Oh God! Somebody please help me!"

Pulling on the door handle, she yelled out in agony at the pain that was ripping through her hand. This door is stuck! "Somebody help me!"

"Hold on! We tryin' to get it open!"

Twila watched in full panic mode while two men worked their hardest to pry the door open.

"Oh Lord! The car is smoking!" A woman yelled from the crowd.

"Oh God!" Twila seethed, feeling as if she was going to pass out at any moment. Glancing back over at Adriana, a fresh flow of tears began to fall fast down her face.

"Adriana! Get up!"

"No...no...no... I got to get out of here." Twila looked out at the frantic faces that stared back at her. Panic and fear gripped her like a glove that was entirely too small.

"This car is getting ready to blow up! We got to get them out of there!"

"I think the girl in the driver side is dead!"

"Oh my God! No!"

"Oh shoot! It's on fire!"

"No!" Twila yelled as she fumbled with the door as hard as she could to get out the car.

Chapter 1

"Adriana, I promise it's going to be okay," Twila said to her best friend, as she flopped down on her oversized beanbag and put her feet up on her desk. "Just go in and blend in with everybody else. Nobody is thinking about what happened all those many months ago. They are on to the next thing."

"Yeah, that's easy for you to say," Adriana huffed. "You weren't the one sent away for murdering the star of the football team. Harriet's High's number one at that."

Twila lowered the volume on her phone and looked towards her bedroom door. She smiled at her small Yorkie, Maddie, as she entered the bedroom and laid down beside her.

"Adriana, you didn't *murder* Kyle so stop saying that. It was an accident, and everybody understands that. You had a problem; made the mistake of trying alcohol and you learned from it. What did the doctors teach you at Holly Grove?"

Twila frowned as she watched Adriana put her head down. Adriana remained silent and stared off into space. The mention of Holly Grove always changed Adriana's demeanor but never to this extent.

"Adriana?"

"Yeah, I'm good," Adriana replied. "Holly Grove is in my past. You know I hated that place and don't like talking about it."

"Yeah," Twila said softly.

"So, what's good with you and Josh? We've been on the phone for almost an hour and I haven't heard you mention him."

"Josh," Twila muttered as she closed her eyes and thought of her boyfriend. They got together soon after Adriana went away and right after the harsh reality that Kyle was gone forever. The memories began to sink into Twila's mind. Not only did Twila have a rough time with her new reality of Kyle's fate but Josh did too. Mourning the loss of his best friend and Twila mourning the loss of her crush, they mourned together and soon their mourning blossomed into a relationship.

"Uh, chick?"

Twila opened her eyes and chuckled. *Okay,* Twila thought quietly. *Let's just change the subject then.* "I don't know. It's like he's different or something. I don't know how to explain it. One minute he's cool and the next, he's yelling at me. I think he blames me for Kyle's dea... the accident," she glanced at Adriana, quickly changing her words. "Since I was in the car that night, I guess."

"Well, don't worry about him. There's plenty of boys who would love to be in his spot."

"Yeah, I guess so," Twila replied while gently petting her puppy. Anxious to get the conversation off Josh and his funny acting attitude, Twila smiled at Adriana. "So, what's good with your parents?"

Adriana chuckled. "They good, I guess. I think my mother is tired of fussing at my dad and finally getting used to the idea that I'm living with him now."

"Yeah, I hope so," Twila said sympathetically.

Squeals and screams from the neighborhood kids echoed through Twila's room from the open window.

"I got it!" One of the kids screamed.

"Dang," Twila mumbled as Maddie hopped up and began to growl.

"Too late!" Another kid called.

"And the barking begins," Twila said as Maddie ran full speed out of Twila's room, down the stairs, and towards the back door, barking loudly the entire time.

"Can't you get Maddie trained or something," Adriana laughed.

"Hush up Maddie!" Twila heard her mother yell.

"Twila! Come and get Maddie!"

Twila shook her head and prepared to get up from the comforts of her beanbag.

"Coming Ma!" She called out.

"Ugh, I wish I could, but I don't have the money for all that. I'm supposed to start babysitting a little girl from my grandma's church, but her father hasn't called me yet."

"Oh," Adriana responded. "You should stop with the babysitting and get a job at Crust. I heard they were hiring."

"Yep, already applied," Twila replied. "I am going to call the manager and—"

"Twila! Get this dog of yours girl! Driving me crazy. Barks at everything and everybody!" Her mother yelled. "Now Twila Marie Anderson!"

"Okay, Ma, I'm coming!" *Just put her in the cage or something*, she mumbled under her breath, surely not to say it loud enough for her mother to hear.

"Maddie, Hush!" Her mother fussed through Maddie's loud barks and the screams of the kids outside.

"I will hit you back later Adriana."

"Okay."

Twila ended the call and jumped up off the beanbag. "Maddie!" She called out as she headed down the stairs.

"Girl, what in the world took you so long? You know this dog worries me with all that barking. Why don't you take her out for a walk? Get her out of here and give my head a break."

Twila grabbed Maddie and moved her away from the back door just in time before the kids made their way back around to Twila's house.

"I don't know why she barks so much," Twila laughed.

"I think your father got this dog for you just to annoy me. A Christmas gift for you but the real gift is to him; millions and millions of headaches for me."

"Really ma?" Twila stammered through giggles. "Daddy knew I wanted a dog, so he got me Maddie."

"Yeah right, go and take Maddie out for a while. Give me a break," her mother replied. "What took you so long?"

"I was talking to Adriana," Twila answered as she grabbed Maddie's harness and leash from the coat rack.

"Alright, Twila. Be careful."

"I know, I know but she's better now, Ma."

"Oh really? Let's just hope so. I haven't forgotten how she tried to pull you into all her mess and the accuse—"

"Yep, I know ma, but she was sick then. Adriana worked really hard and she's better now," Twila said as she quickly placed her dog in its harness and snapped the leash in place, hurrying before her mother went on an hour-long rant about the dangers of Adriana and all the trouble that can and will follow if she wasn't careful.

Chapter 2

"Chile, why don't you find something to do? Grab the bags of potato chips out of the car and bring them in here. Always sitting around doing nothing."

Twila shook her head at her grandmother while she was fussing at her cousin. *Grandma is always trippin'. Always fussing at somebody.* Twila chuckled and walked into the kitchen, glad that her mom wasn't in the way, decorating the place like Twila was five instead of seventeen. *That's mommy for you, always being extra.*

"Twila! Come outside with me. I want to show you what I leaned at practice the other day!"

Twila smiled at her seven-year-old cousin. "Okay, let me see what you got." Walking outside, Twila inhaled the relaxing soft breeze that was blowing in the air before taking a seat on the front porch.

"Look Twila!"

"I'm looking Asia. Go ahead and show me what you got!"

Twila laughed at her cousin as she tried to imitate what she had learned from her Coaches at her cheerleading practice. "Keep going! You'll get it."

Asia sat down in the driveway like she'd just lost her one and only friend.

"Dang, they really get all in their feelings about cheers," Twila quipped before she stood up and stretched. "Come on Asia, lets' go and check on Maddie."

"Maddie! Yay!"

Why did I just say that? Now, she is going to want to stay in my room the entire time she's here; Maddie is going to get tired of her real quick. "Yeah, come one," Twila smiled, anxious to get her cousin off the ground before their grandmother came out and started fussing about it.

"Grandma! I'm going to see Maddie!" Asia excitedly yelled while running towards the stairs.

"Oh Lord! Leave that dog alone gal, you know how bad that dog barks. Don't even get that thang started."

Asia ignored her grandmother and trotted up the stairs anyway, rushing straight to Twila's room. Twila laughed when she heard the faint growl followed by a few barks and then cheerful laughter. Good, Maddie will keep Asia occupied for a little while, so I won't have to pretend her cheers are lit. Walking into the kitchen, she popped a potato chip in her mouth and looked out the window. The wind rustled a bit harder than it had a few minutes before, causing a rustling of the trees. Looking at the trees but not really looking, her mind resorted to Josh. *Josh*, she mumbled silently as she thought about his strange and at times, erratic behavior. *What the hell is going on with him?* Sighing, she grabbed another chip and walked into the living room. *No need to get a headache thinking about him right now. Let me get grandma stirred up*, she chuckled.

"Was sup grandma?"

Flopping down in the recliner, she flipped the chair up and waited for her grandmother to start conversation, knowing that she was getting herself into more conversation than she wanted to when it came to her grandmother. She always for sure had stories to tell from back in the "good ole days", as she called it.

"Hey baby. Yo' momma still at the store?"

"Yes ma'am. I told her that she didn't have to get a lot of stuff because I am only having a few people over."

"Yeah, well, you know yo' momma. She always has to get stuff even when she doesn't need it. You know, she been like that ever since she was a little girl."

And there it is, Twila chuckled internally. The doorbell rang, stopping the long-winded conversation in its tracks. Smiling at her grandmother, Twila pushed her feet down on the recliner and hopped up. Looking out the window, she saw Adriana standing on the porch. Opening the door and looking glancing at her grandmother, she smiled.

"Hey girl."

"Was sup," Adriana said while playfully pushing Twila and stepping in the house.

"Yo chick, you not gonna believe..." Adriana stopped when she saw Twila's grandmother staring at her as if she was the devil himself. *Girl, why you ain't tell me your grandma was here*, she whispered as quietly as she could.

"How are you doing Ms. Shirley," Adriana said nervously.

Twila eyed her grandmother, hoping that she wouldn't say anything out the way to Adriana. She still had a problem with her due to the accident that happened last year. All that happened last year, and my family is still trippin' about it; just crazy, Twila quipped, careful not to say it loud of enough that her grandmother would hear her. She made that mistake of questioning her grandmother's thought process once when she was younger and got slapped to the floor. Lesson learned; she always thinks before she says something that her grandmother would deem disrespectful.

"Fine."

"Uh, that's good," Adriana answered quickly.

Slightly shaking her head, she pulled Adriana's jacket. "Come on, let's go chill on the porch," Twila suggested before her grandmother jumped in her feelings and cussed Adriana out.

"Girl, your grandmother can't stand me." Adriana sat down on the porch, looking behind her.

"I know, she can't," Twila laughed. "Nah, I'm just playin'. She likes you; she just gets in her feelings a lot. That's all."

"Yeah right, she just don't like me."

Twila sat down on the porch next to Adriana and plucked her in the head before looking out into the street.

"Watch dem' hands," Adriana laughed.

"Whateva chick."

"So, was sup?"

"Nothing, ready to get this gathering over with so I can just chill for the rest of the... oh, I meant to tell you about my dream I had the last night. Girl, we were about to get blown up! I was so glad when I woke up form that crazy dream."

"Wow, I'm glad it was just a dream. I ain't got time for nothing like that. Got too much to do to be dying all early."

"Right," Twila laughed but was quickly met with a quick shutter of her shoulders as she thought of just how real the dream seemed. A little too real.

The girls watched a group of kids form to play a game of hide and seek.

"You count!"

"No! I started the last time! You do it!"

"Kids," Twila chuckled. "Arguing over who starts the game." Looking over at Adriana, she frowned. "Aye. Why the long face all of a sudden?"

Adriana sighed deeply and put her head down. "I still have those nightmares; I just can't get away from them. Now that you said something about your dream...got me thinking all over again."

Twila put her arm around Adriana and smiled. "The good part is that they are only dreams. I shouldn't have said anything about mine. My bad."

"Nah, it's all good. It's not your fault that I killed the—"

"Uh uh...nope, we aren't going to keep talking about it. You have to stop saying it that way. You made a mistake and you paid for it, so we are not going to keep saying it that way."

Good, mommy's back, Twila mumbled as her mother's car pulled up in the driveway. *I hate it when Adriana gets all in her feelings about Kyle and the accident*. Twila shook her head as her mother hopped out of the car as soon as she cut the engine; all excited.

"Hey girls! Ya'll come on in and help out with some more balloons."

"Ma, not more balloons, please. We already have-"

"Hush! And come on so we can get this party started."

"Hey Adriana. How are you doing?"

"Hi Ms. Sharon. I'm ok, how are you doing today?"

"Oh, I can't complain."

Walking into the house, they were greeted by a frustrated Shirley.

"Girl! You took long enough! Where in the world have you been?"

"Hey momma, the store was crowded today. You should've come out there with me; get out of the house for a little while."

"Nope, I was just fine right here. No need for me to be going out in that crowd of people shopping for nothing."

There she goes, Twila shook her head. *One suggestion and we have to hear about why it's a bad idea to go and shop.* Twila laughed and looked at Adriana, a look of pure panic displayed all over her face. "Lighten up girl. Come on so we can get this *party* over and done with."

"Ugh, I just don't like coming over when your grandma is over here. I know she just hate—"

"She does not hate you. Stop worrying so much about my grandmother."

"She does and so does your aunts. Are they coming over—"

"Hey! Hey! Where is the cake?"

"Oh no... Twila, let's go outside."

Twila laughed before calling into the living room to speak to her aunts from her dad's side of the family. "Come on girl, let' just go out the back door." The girls walked out onto the back porch and Adriana sighed a huge sigh of relief. Twila trotted down the stairs and gasped at what she saw. Frowning, she watched Josh closely while he was yelling at some boy; a boy who looked familiar but Twila couldn't place him. *Look at him, acting like a fool again.*

"What is wrong with your man?"

Twila kept her eyes on Josh, not sure if she should just watch or actually do something to stop him from making an even bigger fool of himself. *He really has been acting strange. What is wrong with him?*

"I don't know girl; he's been acting a damn fool." Looking inside her house, she saw her mother walk by, holding a plate of cookies, her aunts behind her. *I hope they don't come out here and see that.* She looked back over at Josh and sighed, opting to stay out if it and hoped that he would snap out of his craziness.

"He better stop runnin' up on people like that. That's Tip and he's in a gang."

"A gang," Twila repeated.

"Yep, and they go for that eye for an eye type stuff. Josh better sit his butt down somewhere talking to him crazy."

Twila sat down on the step and put her head down, hoping that Josh would go home instead of coming over to see her.

Chapter 3

"Wassup Twila."

"Hey," Twila spoke to a boy from her social studies class while walking to the bus stop. Twila mainly kept her distance from a lot of the kids who attended her school. Some seemed to have a problem with her because of the accident and the fact that she was still cool with Adriana. To keep herself out of trouble, Twila remained quiet on the bus most days and kept busy reading until the bus reached her school. Standing by herself, her mind wandered to Josh. Maybe he won't be in one of his moods today, she thought. Looking past the crowd of kids, Twila readied herself to get onto the approaching bus. On cue, the bus pulled up in front of them. Twila waited until everybody boarded the bus and she got on after, sitting in the front, directly behind the bus driver.

"Sell out," a girl Twila knew in passing, said loudly. "She should've been up in that place right with her friend."

Twila rolled her eyes and kept her mouth shut.

"Not today!" the bus driver yelled and shook her head. "We not doing this today."

Twila put her ear buds in her ear and turned her music on. Determined to keep her cool from all the kids who wanted to make her life miserable. The kids who blamed her for the reason Kyle wasn't here anymore; wasn't here to win all the football games. Now, our team sucks, they would say. Twila shook her head. They don't care that an innocent person's life was taken, they only care about that fact that he was the one who won football games and put the school on the *map*. Such losers and lames, she whispered as she focused her attention on her music and the trees passing by.

Buzz... Bzzzz... Bzzz..., Grabbed Twila's attention. She quickly opened her bookbag and retrieved her phone. Smiling, she read the text message from her father.

Skating this weekend...

Love you...

Love you too, ttyl, she typed in. Placing her phone back into her bookbag, she focused her attention back on the music coming out of her earbuds and the scenery passing her by outside.

"Why you not driving with that slut of a friend you got?!" Ebony, one of the wannabee hot girls of the school yelled out, causing an eruption of laughter.

"None of yo' business," Twila shot back, rolling her eyes.

"What?"

"You heard me the first time, wit' your lame self."

"Oh, you tryin' to take it there? We can go there?" Ebony stood up.

"Sit down! The bus driver yelled. I will be writing you up when we get to school, Ebony. I want complete silence on this bus! I'm not playin' with ya'll today!"

The bus got silent with the exception of a few chuckles.

"Don't make me pull this bus over. If I have to do that, all ya'll will be getting write-ups." The bus driver looked around through the rearview mirror, daring anybody to speak.

Twila chuckled and turned her music back on. I cannot wait to get this day over with, she mumbled as the kids on the bus remained eerily quiet. Perhaps, too quiet.

The bus pulled up in front of the school. Twila looked up at the big blue sign that towered over the school's lawn. **Harriet High School**: **Home of the Eagles** read in big bold, red letters.

"Alright, when y'all get on this bus later today, I want silence. We are not riding home with a bunch of nonsense," the bus driver reprimanded while the kids stood to get off the bus. Twila purposely waited until all the kids were off before she stood to exit. Grabbing her book bag, she maneuvered out of the seat and walked off the bus. Sighing, she worked hard to tune out all the noisy kids that were, in her opinion, too old to be acting out like they tended to do every single morning. She looked around for Adriana before she headed inside the school. Standing by the door, her eyes focused on the bench that was just recently painted. The number 23, Kyle's jersey number, was painted in red. A small tree blossomed beside the bench and a beautiful hand painted sign that read, In Memory of Kyle Jones stood proudly in front of the memorial. Twila has seen Kyle's memorial more times than she could count, and each time brought a chill. Her mind always wandered to that fateful, rainy night that changed her life, Adriana's, most of the students, faculty, and staff's lives. Not to mention the detrimental lost to the football team.

"Hey girl! Thanks for waiting. My dad was late picking me up today," Adriana said as she waved goodbye to her father. "He had to work overtime again at his night job."

Twila waved at Adriana's father as he blew his horn. "I told you, I got you." Twila said to Adriana as they entered into the school together. "Just don't pay any attention to these haters. You know how everybody is and they don't even talk about what happened anymore."

Adriana gave Twila the side-eye. "Yeah right. I'm sure they are still talking about how I killed the star."

"No... well, just a few but forget them," Twila thought about the fiasco on the bus earlier and rolled her eyes. "What they think or say don't matter. You will be just fine. It's your first day back after a long vacation. It's understandable to be nervous but you will be ok."

Twila and Adriana walked as calmly as possible through the crowded, noise filled hallway.

"Good Morning, girls."

"Good Morning, Ms. Hanks," Twila and Adriana both said in unison to their principal.

"Welcome back Adriana. Please let me know if there is anything that I can do for you. You know I am always here to help you get back in the swing of things," Ms. Hanks smiled and placed her hand on Adriana's back.

"Thank you, Ms. Hanks," Adriana smiled.

Wow, Twila thought. *The new Adriana; all polite. She was never like this before.*

"You girls have a good day."

"Hey! No running! This is school, not the basketball court or football field," Ms. Hanks yelled at a group of boys running and playing in the halls.

Twila chuckled and walked over to her locker. "Okay, girl. Do your thing with this locker. Nothing's changed. I still can't get this thing open most of the time"

Adriana laughed. "Let's see if I still have the magic touch." Adriana turned the lock clockwise, stopped and looked at Twila. "Okay, watch closely," she said slowly.

"Oh, girl stop it and open the locker," Twila laughed.

Adriana giggled as she finished the rotations to snap the lock open. "Ta-da. Still got it."

"Thanks girl. I missed yo—"

"I called you last night. Why you ain't call me back?" Josh interjected, standing in between the girls.

"Uh, she was busy... maybe."

"I wasn't talking to you, Adriana," Josh quipped. "I was talking to my girl."

"I turned my phone off early, Josh. You know, a quick hello would've been nice before you went in on me," Twila rolled her eyes.

"Whateva," Josh mumbled and walked off.

Twila huffed and slammed her locker shut. "See, I told you he's been acting funny lately. Now watch, later today, he's going to be sweet. I don't know what's wrong with him."

"I told you to just forget him Twila. You can do better."

"Yeah, I guess. Do you want me to walk you to your class? You good?"

"Oh yeah," Adriana responded. "I'm good. I will see you at lunch."

"Okay girl and text me if you need me. We can always do a bathroom call."

Adriana smiled and headed to her class. Twila followed suit, walking towards her first and hardest class of the day. Ms. Engelman's math class.

"Ladies! Let's bring it in. You're moving too slow today! Let's go!"

Twila rolled her eyes at her P.E teacher, Coach Snow. Well her name is Coach Gardner, but the students of Harriet High nicknamed her Coach Snow due to her mop of white hair. Yep, Coach Snow was her name and they went with it; behind her back anyway. "Why is P.E even a requirement," she complained as she jogged on the school's track. Looking over at the houses that lined the street, Twila sighed. *I can't wait to get home.* Taking another long sigh, then, taking a long swig of her bottled water she kept with her during P.E class, she continued with her thoughts of anything but her present location. *I wonder what Maddie is up to right now?* Keeping her mind occupied on anything but the run, she thought more about her dog. *I need to give her a bath today; maybe take her to see daddy.*

"Let's bring it in ladies!"

"Finally!" Twila huffed, picking up speed to make it to the locker room as fast as she could.

Standing in line, Twila winced and shook her head as her P.E teacher yelled her words, even though the class was right in front of her.

"Let's get those feet moving a little faster next time!"

"We are right here," one of the classmates said. "Why is she still yelling?" The girls burst out in laughter as they made their way to the locker room.

"Okay, girls. Let's hit the showers! Bus riders, the buses will be late today, so you have some extra time!"

"Ugh! Why does she always yell?" Twila whispered while opening her locker to retrieve her belongings. Ha, so much easier than my other locker; opens with ease, she smiled. *Why can't we just use our own locks with all the lockers here at this school?* Grabbing her bag, she opened it and pulled out her changing clothes and sat down on the blue bench that lined the lockers. *Where did I put my shoes?* Twila rummaged through her bag, seeing everything but her changing sneakers. *Oh, right here.* Pulling the sneakers out of her bag, she placed them on the bench and prepared to take a quick shower before getting on the bus. *I really need to get a car*, she thought as she thought of the noise and the taunting that she faced from the kids who blamed her personally for Kyle's accident. *I will talk to daddy about a car this weekend when we go skating.* Combing through the items in her bag, she looked to make sure she had her deodorant and favorite body spray handy.

"Hey Twila, everything ok? Aren't you going to hit the shower?"

"Uh, yes, Coach Snow, I mean... I'm sorry, Coach Gardner, I was just looking for my shoes. Getting ready to go now."

Coach Gardner laughed aloud, catching Twila by surprise. "Coach Snow, I love it. I know all about my nickname," she laughed. "You kids are funny. You girls just wait until you get my age and have some grey spots on your head. Coach Snow..."

Twila, feeling embarrassed but smiled anyway. "Yeah," she managed to mutter.

"Have a good weekend Twila. See you next week."

"Okay Coach," Twila smiled, remaining quiet until her Coach was out of ear shot. "Oh my gosh! I can't believe I just did that! I cannot believe I called her snow," she laughed. Getting up off the bench, she snatched her bag and headed towards the showers but stopped when she heard a man's voice. Listening closer, she frowned. *This is the girls' locker room. Why is a man in here?*

"Well, you don't have a choice. You either do it or you're off the team," the man's voice muffled.

Twila moved closer to the office's entrance but remained out of view.

"Okay," she heard another voice speak.

"Josh?" She whispered. *What are they doing in here?* Peering through the door, she spotted Josh and Josh's football Coach, Coach Davis. *Why are they in here?*

Come on Josh. Let's get it done before those girls come back through here.

Twila gasped when she saw the needle Coach Davis had in his hand.

"Just a little pinch," she heard him say right before he stuck Josh with it.

www.ingramcontent.com/pod-product-compliance
Lightning Source LLC
Chambersburg PA
CBHW030546200626
46812CB00022BA/1973